Schwartz fell under water as the boat came on him. A roar of water churned down. He came up gasping to see the boat skid sideways, turning to come at him again.

It hit the back of his thigh and buttock so hard it straightened him and he went flat on his face down to the bottom. This time he came up retching silt and salt water.

He could swim for shore; he saw the boat was farther away. A current in the rising tide pulled him to the side and out.

He began his mediocre crawl. Maybe the current would dump him on a beach before he drowned. Maybe after. He tried to keep his spirits up by imagining his body on the beach—the silent crowd, the coroner, the final cost per clam.

He heard the boat roar up behind him. . . .

Also by Irving Weinman
Published by Fawcett Books:

TAILOR'S DUMMY

HAMPTON HEAT

Irving Weinman

FAWCETT CREST • NEW YORK

A Fawcett Crest Book
Published by Ballantine Books
Copyright © 1988 by Irving Weinman

Library of Congress Catalog Card Number: 87-22308

ISBN 0-449-21546-6

This edition published by arrangement with Atheneum Publishers, a division of the Scribner Book Companies, Inc.

Manufactured in the United States of America

First Ballantine Books Edition: May 1989

BOOK I

1

Rita Troost stood on the dune deck below the porch and stretched her short plump arms. Pink. Everything east was a blue rose-pink. The sand was lightest and the ocean bluest pink, except where the surf broke into pink champagne. And over it the sky. The delicate dawn.

She let her arms drop. She really should write a poem or paint this now. The sky's delicate pink dawn. A poem—that needed only pen and paper.

Soon the sun would appear over the Shinnecock Hills. Her "Hamptons sun," she called it. Oh, that was silly, that sort of provincialism, and she really hadn't sunk to that even now in half retirement. A poem . . . Still, it rose from over there, out of the ocean behind Montauk, appeared first east of East Hampton and disappeared into Moriches Bay, west of Westhampton, into the depths.

It was fun like this, occasionally being up so early while Phil and Patsy and the grandchildren—the two, no, two and a half sets of them—were still all asleep back in the little house. And at this quiet hour Plums seemed most its sweet, high-peaked self, like when she and Herb had built it fifty-two years ago.

What would Herb think now? Twenty-five years gone, but even then the dunes had been so less built up.

He'd hate it. Trashy houses, trashy people. She didn't
want to think of all that now, in this pink going to a
pink-blue-gold. A poem. She should. Herb would have
loved how all the planting had taken so well—beach
rose and beach plum grown up everywhere, beach plum
for which they'd named the place, which now blocked
out most of the awful new . . .

Rita looked down the slope. The grasses and fencing
had held well and developed the dunes against spring
storms and even the hurricanes, while so many tacky
get-rich-quick developments had flattened the dunes and
then in turn had been flattened themselves. But not
enough. Tacky places for tacky . . . That was naughty
and she really oughtn't, but they'd spoiled her beach,
those . . .

No. The poem could start—The sky's . . . No. Under
the sky's delicate, pink dawn . . .

Something was wrong by the dune fencing down
there. Another beach party. Not that she minded. She
had been young. And thank God she'd never let herself
lose touch with the young, as had most of her friends.
No, let them use it, let young couples lie under the
summer moon in the warm sand . . .

But not knock down the fencing and—just look at
that—knock about all that grass put in just this spring.
If they'd only realize how the dunes depended on the
grasses. She'd been meaning to have that sign made up
and posted, explaining.

She looked at the battered lower dune, shrugged and
went up to the porch for the long-handled trowel. Not
much arthritis, except for the right knee. Not much at
all, for eighty. If she replanted the grass right away . . .
She bent for the trowel. Plump, yes. But not like some

of them. And not so bad for eighty. Still a womanly
woman, for eighty.

Rita walked slowly down the steps, careful at the
broken ones and those skewed by the shifting sand.

What should follow? Under the sky's delicate, pink
dawn/ The gray sand steps go down . . . Something,
something.

And it would happen where all that grass had been
set in this spring. She stepped off onto the dunes and
went down on her left knee and then onto both. Five or
six clumps. Not so bad, really. She thought she could
see where a couple might have lain. Was there a moon
last night? More a matter of resetting the grass. She
should have worn gloves, but if she were careful . . .

Lovers under the moon. Warm sand, the light sea
breeze . . . Yes, she might . . . Should that be the poem?
Rita smiled. "Love Poem at Eighty." Yes, titles were
important. There, that clump should be all right.

The trowel moved under the sand. She pushed
gently, turning the blade, feeling the textures—sand,
roots and then the harder sand.

At eighty should there be irony? But that wasn't her.
She adored Yeats, of course, but that frenzy for old age
passion simply wasn't her. Only a few more to set. She
looked up. Now the beach had lightened so that away at
its far east end the surf's white mist was pink edged,
like the bloom of silk, from here, like an impressionistic
flower.

Under the sky's delicate, pink dawn/ Something,
something, steps I go down/ To the ghost mist ocean
. . . Or—the ghost mist shore?

Rita looked down. What was that? Not a shoring
timber, not driftwood. No wonder this clump . . . Her

trowel pushed along and pulled back, digging a shallow depression.

Once, in rum-running days, Herb had uncovered three cases of Scotch out here. They'd only had the beach shack then. But this wasn't hard enough. . . . There. The trowel was under it. She wished she'd brought the gloves. There. It wasn't glass, though. There, a loosening at the end. She'd take care for splinters.

She put her hand in. Hard and soft? She grasped and lifted. The sand slid back off her hand and then off the hand she was holding. Then its wrist came out and then the forearm with bits of . . .

Rita let go and pushed up to one knee, using the trowel. She heard herself say, "Under the sky's delicate, pink dawn," as she straightened, shaking on the bad right knee.

She was sensible. She'd stay calm and go up and tell Phil. But Phil was up all the stairs, through the porch, all the way through Plums and down the long drive asleep in the little house out near the road.

She was sensible. She winced and dropped the trowel and started up the dune stairs calling, "Philip! Philip! Something under the sky's delicate, pink . . . pink . . . Someone's . . ." But the poem was decomposing in her head.

2

In the films of California there were those roads endlessly packed with cars, long aerial shots of cars massed and crawling like insects. And they called them freeways, thought Schwartz. What a word. Well, California was another country. No, it wasn't. He looked out at the Long Island Expressway; he could see three miles of cars heading east, and not one of them was moving. Expressway, what a word.

Karen opened her eyes. "Len? Still jammed?"

"Freeways, freedom, the open road, my sweet." He wondered if this was a good time to tell her. No, he'd wait.

"How awful. And I'm so sleepy, I'm no company. But it'll be better after Huntington. It's always better after Huntington. And we're off for the whole summer and to a free house in the Hamptons."

Schwartz nodded. Free was certainly a hard price to beat. And he'd worked and pulled strings to put together accrued leave time and vacation time so that July and August were free. Not quite free. Nearly. He'd better tell her.

She was napping again. Well, later, before they got to this dream house loaned them by Karen's publisher.

The car behind honked.

Ah, yes, he'd forgotten to move up the four-and-a-half foot stretch of highway opened between them and the car in front. Wonderful.

Expressway, freeway. Tom Gallagher's big grin and heavy hand slapping his shoulder. "You're home free," his ex-partner boss had said after the case last spring had reinstated Schwartz as Homicide's hot shot. Home free? By the way of being a successful crooked cop?

He'd hung on through years of quarantine after taking the bribe money, until Gallagher had seen fit to use him again. Nothing was provable; he'd gotten away with it. But Gallagher could sniff bribery as easily as if it were corned beef and cabbage. Like only a clever cop on the make could—Deputy Chief of Detectives Thomas Gallagher with his big Westhampton summer house that no five cops' salaries could buy.

Schwartz looked into the rearview mirror. The car's back seat was full of books and boxes and everything but Jake. One week home from Yale and he'd gone back to New Haven for a summer of coaching Little League —for kids who lived half a mile in distance and light-years in opportunity from Harkness Tower. Jake's free choice. Schwartz was proud. But how would Jake's fine social conscience cope if he knew he was being put through Yale courtesy of a middle-sized cocaine bribe cleverly invested by his pop the cop? Well, it could have been worse; it could have been invested in Krugerrands, it could have been one of the many bribes rather than the one and only. Right? Bullshit.

He shook his head. What a kid Jake was, so self-contained, like his mother. Not twenty and choosing to summer in the slums while Dad plumped for East

Hampton. Schwartz had máde it up for the last game of the freshman season to see his second-baseman son execute a double play of such sweet grace that for a moment, as Jake tagged the base and spun, throwing to first, it seemed as if he floated free of gravity, an all-American Ariel.

A trick, of course. A way of speaking. There was gravity, there was this crawling line of traffic, there was Tom Gallagher manipulating Schwartz's guilt in asking for a little favor—to keep an eye on his nephew Ginger Whelehan, a young detective with the Southampton police on his first case in charge—a routine murder, an old guy mugged and hit too hard out on the beach. And since Schwartz would be around, and since it would be less embarrassing for the young sergeant than if his own uncle was seen helping . . . "Well, what the hell, Lenny, just let him know you're there if he needs you. But only if you want," said Tom with his Kerry—or was it Cork?—charm. So it was his own free choice. Like hell it was.

Karen lifted her head. "Oh, we're moving now. Good."

They were moving at eleven miles an hour. Karen's head dropped into sleep again. He'd tell her when she woke.

That was fifty miles and two hours later, but then she had to read the map she'd drawn and Schwartz had to pay attention. They turned north off the Montauk Highway a few hundred yards after the sign to the East Hampton airport. Scrub oak, pines, sandy driveways and finally the high white wooden fence, just as described.

Karen unlocked the door in the fence and bowed. "Who'll carry who over the threshold?"

"I'll carry you."

"How conventional."

"Yeah, but I like carrying you," he said, scooping her in his wiry arms. He kissed her neck under her thick dark hair.

He stood holding her in a brick courtyard before a house of white wood and sheets of dark glass and sharp-angled roof lines and built-in greenhouses. The court-yard was full of sculpture vaguely recognizable to Schwartz.

"Well," asked Karen, pulling close, "not bad for nothing, is it?"

"That's . . . Isn't that bronze a what's-it, the hermit, you know, the Romanian . . ."

"Brancusi. Yes."

"Wow! Jesus, what a place."

A phone began ringing. Karen slipped down from her husband's arms and went to the door, but by the time she'd found the keys and opened it, the phone had stopped.

It might have been Gallagher's nephew. It was time to tell her.

"Come on, Len. It's even better inside."

"Wait, Karen. Before we go in I have to . . . I didn't get a chance in the car. I'm doing a favor for Gallagher. Sort of keeping an avuncular eye on his nephew, a local cop on his first case in—"

"Damn Gallagher! Why can't the avuncular keep his own eye on him?"

"Well, it mightn't look right—the nepotism. Be-sides, Tom will be back in the city a lot."

"And this is your vacation? I suppose it's homicide. Don't you get enough sleaze-horror in the city? Do you have to lug it out here? Len? Wasn't that what we've worked for—free time? I was supposed to be starting a project on the old Russian painters out here and you—wasn't it Tolstoy? Weren't you going to get bronzed and even more beautiful and reread Tolstoy this summer?"

"Yes, yes. This other thing's nothing, a straightforward mugging manslaughter. And I'm only going to advise—and only if Whelehan, the nephew, wants me to. Don't worry. We'll be the free and serious Sybarites we planned."

"Promise?"

"Absolu—"

The phone was ringing. Schwartz went through the open door. Karen stood on the threshold and looked in to where he nodded and said, "Yes. Yes. I see. Sure. Well, you know where I am if you need me. Right." He hung up.

"The nephew?"

"Himself. Hey, look, the swimming pool out there—"

"So, what did he want?"

"Said his uncle gave him the number and said it was a routine case and he definitely would not be bothering me about it at all."

"Not at all?"

"Not at all, at all."

"So, do I get carried over this threshold too?"

"Sure," Schwartz said, walking slowly around the sofa, rubbing his chin.

"Okay, what is it?" Karen asked, her green eyes narrowing, her right hand moving to her hip.

"Nothing. Just odd, he's so insistent that he doesn't want any help—and the minute I get here."

Karen walked in.

"Hey, I was supposed to—"

"Forget it, Detective. I know when the honeymoon's over."

~~~~~~~ **3**

"Do you agree, Inspector Schwartz?"

Schwartz looked up from the papers on the desk next to the photo. "Call me Len. I'm a friend of the family and this isn't official."

"Right. It's just that it's not often that a high ranking city officer takes any interest in anything out here," said Whelehan.

Ginger Whelehan was young, tall and lean and didn't look much like his uncle Tom. He had the light orange hair of his nickname and the high-cheekboned face of a bird. Or maybe that was the impression of his eyelids, which hung like a hawk's hood. And unlike his uncle, an everyday brown bear, Whelehan was very polite. Schwartz figured a bit of that was political manners; the rest was purely pissed off. He looked back at the photo. The man smiling next to the smiling Whelehan looked familiar. But he couldn't place him.

Like this visit: the whole Southampton station, behind its neat red brick and Main Street pillars, had snapped to attention when Schwartz dropped in unannounced. And the chief, a Captain Beck, had come out all stiff smiled, Uriah Heep with a gun on his hip. And now Whelehan, who'd told Schwartz not to bother, was taking him through the case as if he'd begged for help. Something he couldn't place . . .

"Well, Len?"

"Yes, you have a real suspect—record of muggings, brawls and you say a bad enough heroin habit to make him need cash fast and very bad. On the other hand, he doesn't confess like he has to the other stuff in the past."

"Small stuff, not like this. He's no fool. We'll get a confession, though."

"Ginger, I'm not so sure about his being no fool. The way it took him about four minutes to look from one of us to the other, it seems to me he's a bit dull-witted. And he's been off the junk for a few weeks now, right?"

"Don't let that fool you. These Indians are clever at playing dumb."

"Indian? But he—"

"Looks black. Yes, they've mixed out here until they're mostly black. Probably not a pure Shinnecock left. But if they can show descent they get to live on . . . You know the reservation? Some of the best damned land in the Hamptons, out between the bay and Heady Creek."

Schwartz pushed away the folder. George Plimpton? Could that be a photo of Ginger with the renaissance jock? He stood, offering his hand. "Thanks for showing me around."

"My pleasure. What'll you tell the uncle?"

"If he asks, I'll say it's a routine case with a likely

suspect and a nephew set for a good detective career."

"That's very kind of you. I'm sure Captain Beck would like to—"

"No, really. I'm only on vacation and looking in for Tom's sake. I'll go out the back way into the parking lot. Bye, now."

Outside, Schwartz put on dark glasses against the sun. It was straightforward but . . . Why shouldn't he be photographed with a celebrity? The Indian kid's alibi— "passed out somewhere"—was no alibi but . . . For all he knew, Plimpton's desk sported a photo of himself with Ginger. And the kid's record was bad but . . . Damn it, there was too much that didn't fit. He'd done muggings but hadn't hurt anyone. The violence was all in brawls with other kids. And there was no corroboration that he'd been there, no cincher that he'd crushed in the old man's head. And if, as Ginger said, it had been a junkie's mugging, how had the man been buried so expertly? Junkies who killed for habit cash weren't careful disposing of bodies; they usually managed no more than a few yards' drag into a bush or behind some garbage cans. No, something was very unstraightforward here. And the creepy way he spoke of "the best damned land."

Karen was at the car.

"Hello, sweetheart. How was shopping?"

"You tell me, eagle eyes. I'm wearing my purchase."

"Oh, sorry, Jesus. I was preoccupied. Oh, great shorts. Really. Wonderful, very sexy. Sort of punk Matisse. Lovely. I love your legs—"

"All right, enough contrition. How was your friendly visit?"

"All very cooperative, through clenched teeth. They've got a terrific suspect, a local Indian kid supposed to be a junkie. I think he's probably a bit simple-minded. You can imagine how eloquent he is in his own defense."

"Did he do it?"

"Maybe. Maybe. How should I know? I'm just a tourist here on vacation," Schwartz said as they got into the car. "So what sights are you going to show me—besides those sensational legs?"

"I thought the art village outside of town. Not the Russian place. Students and followers of William Merrit Chase originally, though there haven't been serious painters there for years. And if that bores you we can always go to the Indian Trading Post just across the road."

"Is that the Shinnecock Indian reservation?"

"Yes."

"Oh," Schwartz said, backing from the parking place, "that might be fun."

4

"There goes the bastard now, in the old blue Volvo," said the chief of police.

The two lieutenants and Sergeant Whelehan nodded.

Captain Beck turned from the window. "Thanks for letting us know, Ginger. There is nothing lower than a policeman snooping on fellow officers. I don't care how much rank he has. If there's anything wrong here, which there damn well isn't, we'll handle it ourselves. What the hell do they take us for, sending a city cop out here to spy on us? All right. Pass the word—no one, but no one, is to give that New York kike the time of day. That's all."

Not quite all, thought Ginger, back at his desk. This is a cop who has to be watched closely. And listened to. He smiled, wondered if the pretty wife personally knew de Kooning and ran his finger over the top of the silver photo frame. Not a speck.

5

The sun was burning a small deep hole into the side of his head, but it was better not to change his position. The sweat ran into his eyes so that he had to blink and wipe the sting out with his forefinger, but the squatting would be all right. The important thing, Schwartz thought, was to keep respectfully lower than the old man sitting on the upturned wooden box.

The old man had been stone silent until the badge came out and shone in the sun. A big slow smile came up, opened and broke into laughter. "Hee. You say New York City police and higher up than any these Southampton cops? Oh, thaz good, thaz real good. I like that. Yessir."

Schwartz kept still. He was on the reservation. As Whelehan had said, the reservation had fine land. As he hadn't said, it had unpaved roads and little shacks. It was neat as a pin and poor as dirt, like the house he saw behind the old man on the box, Chief Sun Johnson of the Shinnecock.

"Right. I'm gonna tell you, Mr. Swart. I ain't say he good. He's my own granson and, mister, he a bad boy."

Schwartz heard him say "bad" in three sad syllables.

"But," the old man said, leaning forward, his wrinkled red-brown hands sliding down the faded jeans onto his knees, "he never kill no one. Don't care what *they* say. I *know*."

"Why, Chief?" Schwartz asked, running his hand through his hair as if it could brush away the sunshine.

"Why? 'Cause I'm sayin' John he not very bright but he know what's happenin'. An' the fights he gets into is when there's a fight goin' on, you know, 'cause they go for him 'cause he big and slow. But he wouldn't hurt no one just for money, man."

"Even if he needed a fix?"

The chief leaned back. "Mister, I don' know what they tole you. That John he bad, he do some of that bad shit, but he ain't no junkie. If he look slow that's 'cause he *is* slow. You hear what I'm sayin'? He ain't got all that he might in his head, y'know?"

Schwartz nodded. Sweat ran off his forehead and down his nose.

"An' whatever he do, he never hurt someone he know like old Amboys."

"He knew him?"

"I thought you say these cops go over this with you. Man, they didn't tell you nothin'! Course he knew him. All the blood know Amboys. Victor was a good friend of the Shinnecock. He knew the history. He . . . Why, he helped us all those years ago get this here bit of land free and clear. Now I ain't sayin' John know that, but he know that old man for a friend of his people. You hear?"

Schwartz nodded.

"Well, you hear this. Victor never did have no money to steal. History of these parts, history of the People, that his thing and them books he wrote on it never made him no money to speak of. That for sure."

The sweat was filling the corners of Schwartz's eyes faster than he could flick it away. The squatting wasn't so bad; he could keep that going, but the side of his head and his eyes hurt. He bent his head and blinked. The earth before him spotted dark brown where the sweat fell. "When was the last time you saw Amboys?"

"Well, last spring. Lemme think."

"His death was established as maybe mid-April."

"Yeah, that about it. 'Cause he was here to eat with us just at that big spring tide about then."

"Was he still helping with tribe business?"

"You full of questions, ain't you?"

Schwartz looked up and nodded. He tried to hold his look onto Chief Sun Johnson's, but the sweat made him blink so that those black eyes with their age-yellowed whites seemed themselves to be blinking off and on like a neon sign.

The chief leaned forward again. "Right. I'll tell you 'cause you're not them, man, not the police here tryin' to hang this on my boy John. An' they don' wanna know nothin', man. They don' want nothin' that inter- fere with what they sayin'. Listen, time he die, Victor was onto something big for us. Said he trace old land deeds disappeared a hundred years ago givin' us title to most of the spine of the island out here."

"The spine?"

"The middle, what's called the moraine, where the water come down from." The old man lifted his head back toward the highway.

"And where are these deeds?"

"He didn't say. Victor wasn't a man what would jump into somethin' without it bein' all, you know, all just right. An' now he dead, well, it just one more dream we don' have."

Schwartz nodded. He was dizzy now, but he'd keep lower than the chief if it killed him. He knew it had impressed the old man.

"Hey, listen. I answer your questions. How about you answer one for me?"

Schwartz was trying to look up, but he felt he'd fall over if he did. "Yes, Chief. What?"

"How come you squattin' down there in the sun like some damn fool?"

6

Vladimir Soloff is painting and thinking in Russian of means and ends. The old ones drink their *nalivka* and *kvass*. No, here it's Budweiser. Old fools. A great deal of money can be made with which to move West, where land is so much cheaper. And with that land, in Wyoming, maybe, or in Montana or Utah, and with that

money, the Community of Real Russia will be established—strict and hierarchical, the beginning of the
final counterrevolution.

Kalubin is surprising: one would think a yid would
be impressed with all that wealth. But no, he only wants
the woods to stay as they are. Kalubin is posing as the
link with . . . With what?

Soloff puts the brush down and steps back. The afternoon sun, diffused through the blind across the sky-
light, throws a pale gold over the studio.

The pink area should come up more. He joins his
hands behind him, stands on his toes and pulls his
shoulders back. A small cracking sound, a pleasant
stretching.

Vladimir Soloff is tall and ascetically slim, so that
his strength shows only in the thickness across his
shoulders or in the cable sinew of his arms and legs. But
of course he is strong. One must be to have survived the
war, imprisonment afterward and the release and subtler
persecutions out of prison and then the years in a mental
hospital worse than any prison.

He is strong in body, mind and spirit. He survives,
and with him survives the Russia that ended in 1917 or
1905 or even, yes, with the stupid freeing of the serfs
or, yes, with Czar Peter's destructive importation of
West Europe. And now the irony that because many in
the West know of his paintings—that because there is
still some true Orthodoxy in the West—he has been
allowed out.

Yet so few really understand. Soloff wipes the flat
edge of his long brush across the thigh of his linen
trousers. There is an endless supply of linen trousers, or
silk, for that matter, if he wished. Ah, they none of

them understand. Certainly not John Unicorn Baldock, his patron. The degenerate.

Soloff approaches the large canvas again, putting his face into an area of pink.

Yes, exactly. Kalubin is a link with a degenerate past. Those years before and after the Revolution when cosmopolitan scum were encouraged in painting and poetry and theater. Disgusting, all those *Naums* and *Yakovs* and *Lazars*. Lunacharsky himself, one of those . . .

He squeezes out a coil of carmine and another of cadmium white.

Curse all of them! The glory of Russia thrown away to a rabble. Even the Glebors, who call themselves Believers, swept back on that sentimental tide of memory. Well, let them be, let them be. They are old and cannot last long, now. Or, if needs be, they can be proven not responsible so that the children and grandchildren will take control.

More white. Yes. Let the white come through more under the red.

Oh, certainly many are in it just for the money. But they, too, will serve. God works in wonders. America. Who would imagine that a selfish businessman and a parvenu policeman could be the means for Vladimir Vladimiritch Soloff to establish the Community of Real Russia!

His strong hands work quickly with the brush, short swirling strokes, dabbing back into the paints on the palette, moving to the canvas again. He'll finish by teatime, when Baldock will want him on display for his ridiculous houseguests. "Maestro" he calls him and treats him like a tame ape. Well, well—Baldock too shall serve. Now to finish and attend to the message for Whelehan. He'll go down to tea as he is—the otherworldly artist. Ha! And Whelehan not so clever, not so hard to control. Serfs—all of them have souls of serfs.

He steps back. Yes, the white has done it. Now it is intense. Yes, that indeed is power, thinks Soloff, smiling approval at the wound in Christ's side.

~~~~~~~ 7

From under her sun hat the shade looked like blackness. His voice came out of the black.

"Who's the one who does those dwarf figures?"

She talked into the hat brim: "Kalubin, old Yakov Kalubin. But that was in the twenties and thirties." She took a long breath, smelling hot straw and sweet coconut.

"And those sort of surreal ones, peasanty landscapes like depressed Chagalls?"

"The Glebor brothers. Sasha and Peter. Peter's are the less depressed. But they haven't done any of those since the fifties." She didn't want to go on about the painters.

A cicada began its drone in the pines. Karen looked out. The house was white and glaring. The pool was a blue mirror reflecting the sun. It was too bright, too brilliant. She looked at her naked body. It gleamed a taffy apple red. "Anyway," she said, "they're nothing like Chagall. I'm very scared."

"Of getting sunburned?" Len's voice came from the black, all innocent and unconnected.

It was too hot for this. "I'm scared that the local police think you're spearheading a corruption investigation. What if—"

"If they do, then *they're* scared."

"Yes? And what do police do when they're scared? They take out their little guns and go bang. I mean, when they have one of their own . . . How bad a memory do you think I have? Back in the early seventies when they thought—"

"No relation to this," came the detached voice. "That was the world's biggest police force being held upside down by a couple of very junior cops and having all its pockets shaken out. I'm only keeping an eye—"

"If Tom Gallagher told you to spy on your mother—"

"My mother's dead. And I wouldn't do it. Or other things. This, yes. What is it, Karen? You remember how it was this time last year—occasional lectures at the Police Academy, PR for community crime watch. Gallagher is still my ticket to ride, hooray and alack. And yes, I have actually become interested in this case. Christ, it's clear they're framing a poor half-witted boy. And did you see where he came from, the reservation?"

"I saw it." Behind her closed eyes she saw the sand-dust roads, the shacks, herself walking around in a hot daze.

Len's voice was quiet again from out of the dark: "We were with them, we marched with these people.

Blacks and Indians, the dispossessed. What did we do it for—the exercise?"

Karen propped herself on her elbows. She still couldn't see him. "Don't you come over all pious with me. You sit there in the shadows like some father confessor above it all, when the truth is you're attracted to crime and murder."

"Yes, all true, but that same sophomore sociology should tell you that I go for social motives. This is me, Schwartz the incompleted Ph.D. candidate in sociology, remember? Red Lennie? And so I sense this case also involves a massive screwing of those poor Indians. And if I don't try to help, who's going to—the board of the Meadow Club?"

"The land and the business with the deed?" The bastard was pulling her into it. "But can't they . . . I mean, if there is a fix and crooked police and you're threatening to expose it, won't they just kill you?"

"I don't think so, not l'il ole high-ranking me, especially since they know I'm acting for Gallagher on this, and as far as they know out here in the manicured boondocks of Suffolk County, Gallagher may one day be commissioner."

"Do you think he will?"

"Sure, when I'm made Pope."

"No. It's still no. When all the liberal rationalizing is peeled from your argument, I see raw guilt. Gallagher's hold on you isn't so much that he knows you took the bribe as that he's sure of your guilty feelings. You'll try anything to show him—and yourself—how dedicated a cop you really are."

"Yes. Again, very true. And I'm working on it, but it's a slow process. As to the dangers, I'll be careful, I

won't take risks. And, notwithstanding my other motives, I am getting interested. I'm sure this old guy out
on the beach wasn't killed by this kid and wasn't killed
for money. Maybe we'll go out there and have a look.
All I know is that someone wants this case buried, and
maybe it's not even Whelehan. I haven't figured out
whether he's smart or dumb yet."

"Which means he's smart."

A laugh from the shadows: "Very true. *You're* pretty
smart for a cop's wife, except..."

"In being a cop's wife. Love's old refrain. Are you
feeling better?" Karen asked, turning onto her stomach
and then deciding not to lie on her stomach and continuing to turn onto her back again.

"Yes. The sunstroke headache's gone now."

"Good. So I expect a straight response. Okay, let's
say I see your interest in this case even beyond your
bizarre relationship with Gallagher. But you still have to
promise me that this will also be our time, our vacation.
If not, what's the point of..." Karen stood up and
stretched. "The point of..."

"I promise. Look, I'm actually reading. Feel the
weight of this—solid Tolstoy. And I'm excited about
your project and your getting us a dinner invitation from
the old Russian painters. It'll be wonderful to meet the
last of the old guard, red guard, avant-garde. Isn't this
the holiday spirit?"

Karen dropped her arms and walked into the shade
and sat on Len's lap. "Yes. Except why, my naked
friend, don't you tell your naked wife she's pretty?"

"Because," Len said, letting the big book drop to the
table, "she's beautiful."

She felt his arm beneath her knees and then she held

his neck as he stood and carried her across the decking. Over his shoulder, up in the big oaks beyond the fence, she saw movement, a flash like a lens catching the sun. No, no. That was just her fear.

Karen pulled closer to Len and shut her eyes against the light. Perhaps he'd think she shivered with desire.

~~~~~~~ 8

It was dinner with the Russian painters. It was two old farmhouse rooms that had been made into one. It was long and had walls of tongue-and-groove cherry wood, and it was lit by kerosene lamps and full of paintings and people with names like Yasha and Masha and Sasha and a very beautiful Natasha. Schwartz took another iced vodka. Neat. Did he mean "nice"? Nice, neat. It was ice, but when he swallowed it turned to fire. He thought about desire because it caused desire or was that ice? No, that was Frost. That's it, he was remembering a poem.

"How do you like the vodka?" asked the tiny old woman with bright blue eyes.

"Neat . . . it's very nice," Schwartz said, thinking that "neat" was only slightly less revolting a word than "nifty." He might ask Madame Kalubin where was the inarticulateness of yesteryear and answer right here in his neat, nifty head, but instead he smiled.

"We flavor it ourselves with special herbs. Very Russian. Come here, I show you something else very Russian to eat. Come, please."

He followed the bun of her fine white hair through elbows and hips of these Olyas and Alexeis and Karens to the wall with the three unmatching sideboards. It was like a furniture store except with all the paintings it was like a Kalubin show at a gallery except with all the food spread out it was more like the Ukrainian deli down on First Avenue near Seventh. And everything looked so delicious.

Almost everything. Anna Kalubin held a small plate next to a large glass jar.

"Look, I give you this. Is special." She held out a fork on the end of which hung, mottled brown and white, puckered and dripping thick mucus, a . . .

Schwartz turned away his head. "Thank you. No, Madame Kalubin." His eyes stopped on a painting of a green and red horse with yellow ears and a Blaue Reiter.

"You please call me Anna or Anushka. At my old age I want no more formality. Here. Eat. I know looks horrible, but try. Please, for me."

Schwartz looked at the woman. She was well into her nineties, smiling and beautiful.

"Please," she repeated. "I am so old—you must. I tell you how old. Is true. When I was baby my family went to Crimea for holidays. And old man from next estate, villa, you see, sat me on lap and rocked. I remember. Big, with long beard. You know who? Is true. Was Lev Tolstoy."

"Really?"

"Really, of course. So now you try pickled mushroom. Your beautiful wife have some before. She like. We take from woods ourselves."

Schwartz shut his eyes and decided to swallow it whole, but it caught on a tooth and he began chewing, finding it something between a truffle and an oyster, though *what* between them, he couldn't make out.

But it was fine and iced vodka and getting wonderful, that lovely Natasha smiling at him, and then they were all seated at the long, long table—three tables together like the sideboards in this wonderful room, and he was at one end near Anushka and was smiling at the other end where Karen was sitting between the Glebor brothers and looking sternly back at him not realizing, he guessed, what a wonderful time he was having. And all the Kalubin and Glebor clans sat down both noisy sides of the food- and wine-filled table. And, yes, another iced vodka would be fine.

Sasha Glebor was telling Karen he was older than his brother Piotr. Piotr yelled back that Sasha, as usual, was wrong.

"Who's wrong?" Schwartz asked Anushka.

Anushka turned to her old husband and yelled into his ear in Russian.

"Both." Kalubin grinned. His mouth was full of pink and black windows. "As usual, both of them are wrong."

Schwartz was thinking about this when old Piotr began tapping a knife on his wineglass for attention. "Excuse, please. For these guests, I tell story of when I introduce famous poet Mayakovsky to America. Nineteen twenty-four, a big hall in New York is full of important people want to see brilliant Russian poet and I give very serious introduction to these people. Men in tuxedos, ladies in gowns and jewels, and so Mayakovsky stand up and after applause he begin say, 'Good evening, fockers!'"

Laughter from the sides of the table, cries of "Not that one again, Grandfather." Schwartz laughed.

Sasha Glebor shouted, "Is as usual completely confused. Is not my brother, is *me* introduce Mayakovsky to America. Is, excuse me, 1927, not '24, and Mayakovsky say, 'Hello, cocksockers!'"

Laughter, shouts of "Oh, Father," and "Really, Grandpa!"

Yasha Kalubin turned to his wife. "*Shto? Shto?*"

Anushka yelled in his ear again.

"Listen, my friend." Kalubin leaned across his wife toward Schwartz, the top of his bald knobbed head gleaming with sweat. "Glebors are wonderful painters and dearest friends but are also sensational liars. *I* am introducing Mayakovsky in New York in '26. *They* are maybe introducing poet Esenin a few years later. But only maybe."

"Esenin? Esenin?" shouted Piotr at the other end of the table. "That man drink anything. He drink . . . in my studio he drink turpentine."

"Turpentine nothing!" shouted his brother, Sasha. "Turpentine like champagne to him. Esenin completely crazy. Drink diesel oil."

"Terrible man when so drunk," yelled Piotr.

"Yes, too much drink can ruin anything," Karen said. "Don't you think, Len?"

Schwartz found this very funny. Karen was glaring at him. He put his hand gently onto Anushka Kalubin's ninety-five- or ninety-six-year-old hand. He told her she was a very beautiful woman. She smiled. He smiled. Down the table that beautiful Natasha smiled. Karen was still not smiling.

Oh, well, the pirogi went very nicely with the iced vodka, and vice versa. And it was a wonderful dinner party.

"It was, wasn't it?" he asked her again as Karen turned the car in the clearing and started the drive through the woods.

"Oh, yes. Especially your drunken clowning. That was terrific, Leonard. That duck-walk dancing of yours should set me up wonderfully for the research I'd hoped to do with Kalubin and the Glebors."

"Think I'm drunk? Think my *kazatchak* was drunk?"

"I know damn well you're drunk. You pride yourself on never asking me to drive and you did just now even though you know I've had a few myself, Officer. So, yes, you're blind damned drunk."

"Karen, pull over, please," he said quietly.

"Oh, great," she said, stopping the car beneath a large white oak. "And now you're going to be sick."

"No. Now I'm going to look at these beautiful woods and tell you what I think I've learned about them. I asked you to drive so that anyone would think I was drunk, like they thought at dinner so that they talked and argued thinking I wasn't paying—"

"Who are you talking about?"

"The children, the grandchildren. Old man Kalubin too. There's an enormous family fight going on about this place. From the bits and pieces I heard, it still belongs to the old folk, the Kalubins and Glebors. And they want to keep it just as it is. But the children and grandchildren are split. I heard them mention development rights and offers to buy. Some were for it, others against."

Schwartz looked out the window. The air was cool

now and filled with sweet scent and the steady trill of crickets. "Beautiful. About a thousand acres here, I gathered. Must be one of the largest undeveloped, un-farmed tracts left."

"Yes, very pretty. And?"

He turned to Karen and put his hand onto hers, which still held the steering wheel. "I'm not drunk, and whose woods these are I think I know. Just possibly this is the land that Chief Sun Johnson said was taken from the Shinnecocks."

Karen looked straight ahead. "And so it's possibly connected with that death on the beach?"

"Possibly."

"Still, you had no right to risk my good relations with these people. I was their guest and you were mine, and . . . Oh, that's pompous, I suppose. Well, what else did you pick up in your convincing drunk act—besides that pretty woman?"

"No, that wasn't . . . Well, I heard a few of the Kalu-bins speaking of Soloff, the dissident, how he couldn't be there tonight."

Karen nodded. "Yes. He stays out here somewhere. Has patrons."

"I've seen some TV interviews. A reactionary nut case if you ask me. He makes Solzhenitsyn look like a Socialist, with that new Russia or real Russia business. Is he as good a painter as they say?"

"Possibly." Karen paused. "You know, Len, you could have told me you were putting on an act. I might have been able to enjoy myself then."

"It wasn't planned; I sort of extemporized. I don't think I loused up your research, but I was out of line

and I'm sorry. I'll make up for it. Let's go home and go
skinny-dipping in the pool. Yes? Yes?"

Karen kept looking straight ahead so that it was difficult to see her expression. She started the car and said,
"Possibly."

9

Kitty Gallagher set the tray of iced tea on the table.
"Here you are. There's more fresh mint in the glass if
you want, Lenny. I'm sorry Karen couldn't make it."

"So is she. She's doing research for a project out
here."

"Another prizewinning art book?"

"Yes, sure."

"Well, next time. It would be nice for the four of us
to get together, like in the old days."

"Yes, it would, Kitty," Schwartz said, half rising as
she returned.

"Sure you won't join us?" asked Tom.

"Too hot. You know how I burn. See you later. Yell
if you need more tea." Kitty bounced up the semicircles
of brick stairs, a strong plump woman in her early fifties
in cutoff chinos.

Schwartz sighed. Tom had quite a code worked out

with Kitty: of course there was plenty of shade down here under the table's big umbrella.

Gallagher pushed a glass toward Schwartz, took his own and shook in a packet of artificial sweetener with a sour nod. The little alligator on his blue knit shirt lay horizontal on a heavy pectoral; the blue swelled over his big belly as he breathed in. It stretched on his biceps when he raised his glass and said, "To the good old days."

Schwartz lifted his glass and drank. "Yes," he said, "we had some."

"We still will. Listen, we'd like you and Karen to come to our annual summer bash next month. Friends, some department people and others I'd like you to . . . Like a formal welcome back to—what do they say— the fast lane, the inside track?"

"Thanks. We'd love to."

Schwartz pulled a sprig of mint from the glass and chewed it. It was sweet and bitter at the same time.

"Well, now, Lenny, what do you think of my nephew?" Gallagher leaned back so that he showed the madras plaid of his Bermuda shorts. They looked slightly ridiculous on his thick, scarred legs.

Schwartz took the mint from his mouth. "I think he's a bright crooked cop."

"Jesus Christ! You don't mince words."

"Want me to, Tom?"

"No, no. Okay, but aside from the 'takes one to know one' bit, what makes you think so?"

"If it comes to that," Schwartz said, looking to where the large lawn sloped down toward a dock, "just how many feet of Westhampton waterfront do you have here? The place seems bigger than I remember."

"Okay, wise-ass. Let's just keep it professional."

"Good. Well, for openers, your neph—Detective Whelehan has charged a half-witted Indian boy who knew and liked the victim. Then there's confusion over his being a junkie or not. But either way, the suspect couldn't have done the very neat disposal job on the old man. Next, a lot of pertinent information hasn't been entered into the case record—the kind that would indicate very different motives than a random beach mugging. Something involving land and lots and lots of money. And none of this has been difficult for me to find out. It's as if the case had been thrown together, not just sloppily, but with the kind of arrogance that comes from knowing you can get away with anything. Professional enough?"

"Yeah, yeah, but what do you *know* about this land business?"

"Not much, yet. I may get over to County Records in Riverhead. It looks interesting, even if Whelehan's not involved. But I think he must be. So do you. Right?"

"I don't know. All this is what you're telling me."

"Cut the crap, Tom. You're the smartest cop I know. Smarter than me. You supposed something was up and didn't mind using eager little me to check it out. I know —from those good old days we just toasted—how adept you are at covering that broad Hibernian beam of yours."

"It's a good thing I'm fond of you, Lenny. It's your vocabulary, I think. I ask myself how many hebe cops would know 'Hibernian' and come up with only you. So damned Harvard smart. Extraordinary how smart. Only trouble, I say to myself, about my ex-partner Schwartz is that he's too damned smart."

"I'm glad we're keeping all this so strictly professional, Tom. If we weren't, I might tell you of the sneaky feeling I have that if it turns out your nephew *is* bent, you'll see to it that this informal investigation of mine is buried even better than old Victor Amboys was."

"Oh, you're wrong there. But we'll both have to wait and see. Won't we?"

"Sure, Tom. Meanwhile, what do I get from you beside your blessing?"

"It's not official. If it comes to that, we have no actual jurisdiction. But let's say that besides me there's some other support for your looking into this—local support and some other."

"It must be very comforting to be so well connected."

"It's hard work. A pain in the ass, actually. But it sure as hell beats getting away with a coke bribe and then running scared."

"Now, boss . . ."

"I'm sorry, Lenny. That was out of turn. Look, this isn't so nice for me, and so you're doing me and everyone a real favor by looking into it. Really."

Gallagher took a deep breath and let it out so that his broad shoulders sagged. He smiled at Schwartz and said, "If this gets big or tricky or, for Christ's sake, dangerous, you let me know and I'll try to help. I like you, Lenny. You really piss me off, but I like you."

Schwartz drank, set the glass on the tray and stood. "I think I'll leave in this glow of blarney brotherhood. Thanks for the tea. And thank Kitty. I'll go out through the garden."

"Right. Thanks, Lenny. Keep in touch." Gallagher waved a big hand and let it flop onto his thigh. He watched Schwartz cross the lawn and disappear through the gate set into the high box hedge. Then he heard the car go off.

He picked up the cordless telephone and poked at it with his thick index finger. "Hello?" he said. "Ginger? This is your Uncle Tom."

10

They'd taken the car, a Dodge convertible left by Karen's publisher, down to the beach. Schwartz didn't like the car. It was slick and new and mean, dodgy like the worst of summer visitors. But, he explained, it was perfect for this expedition. Karen liked the car. It was breezy and useful. She asked if his explanation wasn't creating more mystery.

"Yes, but sometimes creating it is part of solving it. I mean, making a world in which the crime fits. I mean . . . Anyhow, if a detective can't be mysterious, who can? Right?"

"No, Len. Yes, Len. Every third word makes sense, Len. Is the egg salad ready?"

An hour and a half later they sat eating egg salad sandwiches and drinking beer at the bottom of the dunes below Rita Troost's house, out on the beach at Quogue. "Maybe slightly trespassing" had been Schwartz's professional judgment on locating there rather than at Karen's choice "between mean low and high tides," a phrase, as she put it, not only enshrined in memory but so devotionally rubbed as to be almost indecipherable.

Schwartz was explaining, no junkie or mentally retarded kid could have done so neat a burial. "Look— the body would have to be dragged up there over at least three dune barrier fences."

"Could Amboys have been up there?"

"Yeah. I checked out the weather against Sun Johnson's recollection. There were big spring tides and not much of a beach left. So he could have been up there, but there's still the matter of those fences. And meeting a mugger in that sort of weather?"

"Maybe he sat down up there to take shelter from the wind."

"Or was even up there on that deck." Schwartz pointed. "See the round lady in the big blue hat?"

"You think that's the woman who found the body?"

"Yes, it's probably Rita Troost. Let's say hello. After all, she's been nice enough not to notice us and call the cops."

"Maybe we should dress."

"No, bathing beauty," he said, showing the badge wallet in his hand. "This is all the cover we need."

They started up the dune stairs in their bikinis, Schwartz calling "Hello" and "Hi there" with great cheer.

The woman on the deck turned. "Hi. Who's that? Come on up; I can't see in the glare."

Under the big straw sun hat she wore a light blue half-smock over wide-legged housepainter pants. Her hands were in her pockets and her jaw stuck out.

"All she needs," Len whispered, "is a cigar to be Churchill."

"Sexist. All you need is a few divisions to be Stalin."

"Tsarist. You could have at least called me Roosevelt."

"Hello! Are you friends of Phil and Patsy? Nice to see you. I'm Rita Troost, Phil's mother. Have I seen you at Plums before?"

Schwartz opened the badge wallet. "Mrs. Troost, Detective Inspector Schwartz. My wife, Karen. We were picnicking and I thought I'd ask you some . . . I'm fascinated by this Victor Amboys business."

"Oh? How odd. Do sit down. I was just doodling. I write poetry. Rita Troost. I have been published by the Houghton Mifflin company. Please sit."

They sat on a bench built around the deck. Rita Troost sat in a chipped metal garden chair.

"Why odd, Mrs. Troost?"

"Rita."

"Oh, yes. I'm Len. Why odd?"

"What? Oh, yes, police. Well, I thought all that business was over. The horrid Indian arrested, you know." She turned to Karen and smiled. "My dear, I'm sure we've met."

Karen smiled. "Perhaps. I sometimes give talks."

Schwartz said, "Rita, I'd like to get the story one more time. The first you knew of it was when you were digging and found the body."

"Yes. Of course."

"There was nothing before—nothing you remember from the spring, around mid-April, when Amboys was . . . when it happened?"

"No. How could there be? I wasn't here."

"But don't you sometimes come out for weekends in the spring?"

"Yes, but not this April. I was traveling. A splurge —Sumatra and Java for two months. March and April. I wasn't out here until at least mid-May. Is it Karen? What sort of talks do you give?"

"Oh, on art."

"Karen Schwartz, Karen Schwartz," said Rita, thinking.

"No, Karen Walker."

Schwartz caught Rita's attention. "I'm confused," he said. "How is it the police report has you saying you were refixing damage done to the dunes in April? How did you know?"

"Well, it was Phil, of course. He spends time here. He'd told me of the big tides and storms and said we'd had some dune damage and showed me where it had been replanted. We have to care for these dunes, you know. They're our . . . Not Karen Walker the art historian?"

"Yes."

"My dear! I just love your book. Of course, I have it inside. And we have met—at a luncheon talk you gave last winter at the New York Historical Society. I'm on the board. Oh, I'm so—"

"And this damaged area was where you found the body?"

"Yes. You know why he put it there, don't you?"

"No."

"Well, it was obviously an easy place to bury poor Victor, some place already dug up. Don't you think?"

"I don't know. But what was Victor doing here? A friend of your son, was he?"

"No. No, we knew Victor, of course. Everyone—I mean, all the older families—knew Victor. He was a local historian. Very knowledgeable. But I don't think anyone knew him socially. He was very . . . Well, not exactly reclusive, but he certainly had rather surprising acquaintances, real lowlife, considering. I mean, well, you know 'Amboys' is an anglicized version of 'd'Amboise,' don't you? His family went back to knights of Charlemagne."

"Ah, I thought I recognized the name. But I don't know any of the d'Amboises, myself." Schwartz turned to Karen and put his arm over her shoulder. "We don't know the d'Amboises, do we, darling?"

"Not even the Amboys, dear."

"Not even the Australian branch, the Perth Amboys?"

Rita Troost stood. "That's very droll and I suppose I deserved it. But perhaps not just here and now."

"Rita, I'm sorry," Schwartz said. "But from what I hear, Victor was a nice guy and liked by the Shinnecocks. And so I don't see how this Indian kid, who by the way isn't so much 'horrid' as mentally retarded, could or would have done it. And, to be frank, I don't see why Amboys's life was such a blight on his family tree."

"What a curious policeman you are," Rita said, with a smile.

Karen asked, "Full of curiosity, or do you mean odd?"

"Both. Decidedly both. What about some lemonade or something stronger up on the porch?"

"Well," said Karen, looking at Len, "our things . . ."

"Oh, bring them up. I'd be so honored if you'd autograph your book. It must be wonderful to be married to so brilliant a woman. And so beautiful."

"It is. It's wonderful. It's full of wonder. We'd love to spend a little time, and I promise there'll be no more nasty police questions. It's too beautiful here. This house, the view. . ."

"Oh, yes, the house is sweet. You'll see. But the view. Well, we do try to keep it fine for everyone, but it's a struggle, as you can see. That house next door—what a monster, and last summer there were only dunes. It went up so fast! And look, over there. We call those awful circular condos the 'Jelly Doughnuts'—they're so badly built and so ugly."

"But how do you stop them?"

"Oh, we help inform public opinion. And zoning, of course. Zoning is very serious business out here. We've always been involved. Phil—he's in New York now, but you must meet him—my son Phil's chairman of the township zoning board."

"Yes, I'd like to meet him. We'll get our things and see you up on the porch."

At the bottom of the steps they shook out their beach towels.

"Very impressive, Len. I've never seen you actually snoop before."

"Oh, you noticed, did you?"

"Yes. I assumed it was your work rather than interrupting out of jealousy at her interest in me."

"Maybe a bit of both. But I'm not so bad on the job, especially once we're away from that perfect house in East Hampton with its perfect pool and all those perfectly important Warhols and Stellas and Dines. All that perfect investment."

"Bob has a fine eye. And his house and pool and even that gauche little Dodge are pretty generous and so what on earth are you complaining about?"

"You know me—not really complaining. It's that

this case is more than Gallagher let on. He knew. He knows. It's getting interesting. The shit—he knew it would hook me."

"Just as long as the hook doesn't go too deep. Come on, let's get back to Rita. I'll bet she also dabbles in painting and wants my sincere opinion."

"Rita's okay," he said.

"Of course she is. She's great, she's a fan, and anything's better than your moaning, your kvetching."

"You're getting to pronounce that perfectly," he said.

"Why not? You give me plenty of practice."

Schwartz said, "Ho-ho," and went up the stairs thinking that, yes indeed, he would very much like to meet Phil Troost and have a nice little talk on local land use, but then Karen pinched him hard on the behind so that he yelped and ran up before her.

11

Schwartz was relaxed. Everything was better, simpler, since the good long talk with Karen, the kind they hadn't had for months. What had been wrong with him, so quick to seal himself away from the one person he really needed? Well, never mind. They'd talked—without yelling—and he hadn't made jokes. And talking with Karen made him understand how he was confusing this case with his own problems of guilt and insecurity. So when she said that even a slightly more objective view would show him that both law and justice would be best served by turning over his findings to a formal investigating authority, he knew she was right. He already had enough evidence of a shoddy cover-up in Amboys's murder to force a formal investigation. So he'd relax now and enjoy himself. And if he would, so would Karen.

He thought of how that night after their talk they'd gone to bed feeling sweetly chaste. They turned off the air-conditioning because, really, they both hated it, and then they lay too hot under the sheet, so they pulled it off and lay still, side by side. Then he saw the moonlight cross the bed, a slow pale gold edge that washed over Karen until her body shone, mysterious in the ordinary movement of her breathing in and out.

And they'd turned in toward each other at the same time, touching and taking each other into their mouths with kisses sucked in and the licking of tongues. And he thought of how when he entered her he'd held the top of her head with one hand and the flesh under her hip with the other so that slightly kneeling he moved her or was it her moving him so that he couldn't tell, it seemed, where they were different or the same. And then he'd slept and woke relaxed.

Schwartz set down the book of Tolstoy stories. Somewhere out there his lovely Karen was collecting blueberries and huckleberries. These were wonderful woods, and the Kalubins and Glebors were so good to make them welcome. Sweet people. His hand touched the book cover. Tolstoy had asked, "What is to be done?"

Yes, keep the land for everyone to use—to use well and enjoy. Not to own. He thought that, after all, as Tolstoy had put it in that marvelous folk story about land greed . . .

"How much land does a man need?"

Schwartz looked out at the woods. Exactly. How much . . .

What? His hand dropped from the book onto a pinecone. Wait a minute—*he* hadn't said that. But it was exactly as if someone . . . No, he wasn't going nuts; that was just his spirit moved in imagination . . .

"Friend, how much land does a man need?"

Behind him.

Schwartz turned. A tall man stood behind him. He had a long black and white beard and he wore a Russian peasant shirt over a pair of baggy trousers tucked into soft black boots.

Yes, he was going mad. Who . . .

"Leo Tolstoy," said the ghost of Leo Tolstoy.

Its aghast beholder murmured, "Leonard Schwartz."

"No, no. That was *said* by Tolstoy. My name is Soloff. Vladimir Soloff." And the man gave a charming smile and short bow.

"Excuse me. I've just been reading Tolstoy and was thinking the words you spoke so that when I turned I thought . . . Very silly, but you looked like . . ."

"Like Tolstoy? Yes, I know." The man laughed. "I do and I admit I cultivate it, somewhat."

"What I was actually thinking," Schwartz said, as the man came to where he sat, "was how awful it would be if all this beautiful land ended up in the hands of the developers."

"Really?" asked Soloff, squatting beside Schwartz.

"The question seems how much land do these very few old people need, people who can barely use it now. Don't you think, excuse me, that it is a bit selfish? Isn't that what Tolstoy meant?"

Schwartz said, "I'm no expert, but wasn't Tolstoy's story set in what was then the limitless lands of the steppes? Wasn't he thinking of avarice? I don't think he had in mind justifying a development of second or fifth vacation homes starting at four hundred thousand or more, destroying the little bit of woods left out here. On the other hand, if you were thinking that it might be used as land for everyone . . ."

"You are serious?"

"Or as land for cheap decent housing for the local poor . . ."

"Ha!"

"Or for the itinerant potato pickers. Or maybe just given back to the Indians?"

"With apologies, sir. I do not understand. Here this wonderful country of yours flourishes only because men are allowed to develop ideas into realities and can live accordingly. Where I come from this is not possible and so it is a great prison."

"Yes, but it's a prison maybe because people can't do enough, not because they can't be too greedy. Still, excuse *me*, I don't quite see why you—of course I know who you are—should be so interested in land that isn't yours, especially since you seem such a believer in the sanctity of private ownership."

"I have friends here. Fellow Russians. And I do not like to see them robbed by the misplaced sentiments of the slightly senile. It hurts me to speak of these fine old painters here like this, but it is true. And it isn't greed.

Perhaps someday you will learn of my ideas for a new type of land . . . Ah, but let us not argue, my friend. You say you know of me. You are in the world of art?"

"No, but my wife is. She's an art historian. Karen Walker."

"Oh, of course. I've been told. She is to visit my good friend and patron John Unicorn Baldock. You know, Baldock Island. I stay there and work sometimes. I think, is it not correct, that your wife will be going over there because Unicorn has the finest Kalubins and Glebors, some never publicly shown. And so this is how she . . . Yes, yes. And how you come to . . ."

"Yes?"

"You are a police officer, I hear."

"Yes, but I'm not working. Just out here on vacation sitting in the woods and reading Tolstoy."

Soloff stood. Karen was emerging from the trees before them carrying a large plastic bowl.

"Blueberry and huckleberry pie tonight, Len." She stopped and looked at the tall bearded man.

"Vladimir Soloff, madam." He bowed and held out a big bony hand.

"Hello. Karen Walker. I've seen only a few of your paintings in New York. I found them very powerful."

"God's power, not mine, I believe."

Schwartz looked down, smiling. What a smoothie! A small line of ants was struggling to bear off a large dead wasp, a yellow jacket, at the corner of Schwartzthumb and Tolstoy. Now Karen and Soloff were speaking of Baldock Manor House and how much she looked forward to . . . And likewise he's found her Cézanne-Monet book so brilliant. The ants were detoured at Pinecone, but they'd get there. Jesus! How it came up pounding his heart, constricting his veins—how goddamned physical his jealousy, lugging him away.

"Len?"

It was Karen, repeating, "Len, we have time for Vladimir to show us some mushrooms, don't we?"

Schwartz sprang up. "Of course. It's quite the thing in Russia, I believe."

"Whole populations, sir. I know of whole populations who survived in great part because of mushrooms, during the war. Come, it is my pleasure to show you."

They walked on a sandy path through the pines. Schwartz wondered how the ants were getting along. Karen was asking Soloff about his good English. He was saying he'd first studied it before the war.

"You don't look . . ." she said, and stopped with an embarrassed smile.

"Thank you. I was seventeen at the end of the war. I had been fighting for four years. Now. Where there are mostly pines, it is not so good for mushrooms at this time of the year. But in here where there are oak trees and the forest is mixed, it is good. Look."

Soloff stopped and picked up a long wicker basket from behind an oak. "This is what I've found."

He took two large white mushrooms from the basket and handed one to Karen and the other to Schwartz. "This is very delicious," he said in his good American accent, only the slight roll of his "r's" and the formality and the clipped word endings marking him as foreign.

Schwartz said it looked like a big version of an ordinary mushroom.

"Smell," said Soloff.

Karen said, "Delicious, like almonds."

"That's right. This is *Agaricus*, and it is the wild cousin of the ordinary large cultivated mushroom. But much more taste. Now look at how the base comes out. It is called 'abruptly bulbous' *Agaricus*. From now until October you can find this."

"I think I could identify this one," said Schwartz.

"Aha. Wait. Come, let us walk."

They went on through the oak dapple, Soloff leading, then Karen, then Schwartz. Schwartz put his hand on the back of Karen's shorts. She pushed it away. Schwartz wondered if the yellow jacket had been absolutely dead. It had looked very elegant, very striped and well dressed compared to those proletarian red ants. Ahead of them, Soloff had stopped.

"Aha. Aha. Here, in the grass near the oak roots."

Schwartz moved up beside Karen. At their feet were three more large *Agaricus*. He bent to pick them but stopped, seeing Soloff's waving hand.

"No, no, my friend. This is not what you think."

Soloff dug around the base of the mushroom with a small trowel and pulled it up whole, shaking off the sandy soil.

"You see the difference? Look, only at the base. See how this has a cup around its base?"

The one Schwartz held had a bulbous end, continuous with its stem. Soloff held one ending in a little sack, as if the stem grew from a short pale bag.

"And what's that?" Karen asked.

"Something one must never eat—*Amanita virosa*. It is called 'the destroying angel' and is one of the few truly deadly mushrooms. I have known someone die of this. It is so often fatal. And a very terribly painful death."

Soloff set the mushroom down and wiped his hand in clumps of grass. "So," he said, "it is so important to know exactly. And not only these two; others, like the very nice chanterelle and the one you call here the jack-o'-lantern, which looks like it but is bad, although not deadly like the destroying angel."

They put the good mushrooms into the basket and walked on. Soloff spoke of spore prints and eating small amounts of safe mushrooms you were trying for the first time.

And Schwartz, despite himself, enjoyed the big man's enthusiasm as Karen and he talked of painting and mushrooms and galleries and art critics and patronage and mushrooms.

"I think we really should go now. It was so nice meeting you, Vladimir," Karen was saying, standing in the late afternoon shadow on the edge of the woods.

"It will be so nice to see you soon on Baldock Island. Please, let me share a dish I cook from these beautiful mushrooms? It would be an honor."

"Thank you," said Schwartz, "but we really have to be getting home now."

"Yes, yes, of course. I mean that Natasha can take it to you. Natasha, the Kalubin granddaughter, also a good painter. Very lovely girl. She remembers you. She's going to East Hampton tonight. If I may give her your address. If that would be all right. It would give me so much pleasure to share this. For this nice afternoon with you."

"Yes" and "Yes, very nice of you, of course" came from Karen and Schwartz.

They shook hands and watched Soloff move back into the woods with long strides.

"What a passionate character!" said Karen as they drove out onto the Noyack Road.

"He is."

"You hate him."

"No. He's charming. But his politics! A little talk we had earlier, while you were berrying." The word echoed in his mind as "burying."

"It's hard to imagine he's been through all that—the war, prison, all the other suffering. And he still looks so . . . so . . ."

"Handsome?"

"No. Lord, no. He's ugly, really."

"Attractive?"

"Yes. Attractive," Karen said, her hand sliding onto his thigh. "Thanks, Len. I was wondering what he was. You've hit it. Yes, attractive."

"Ha, ha. I'm not one bit jealous. But keep your hand right there on my thigh, say, from now until September."

Schwartz began pumping his foot up and down on the accelerator so that the Volvo surged forward and slowed, surged forward faster and slowed, ending with a great long surge forward.

"Len, what is all this?"

"The automotive analogue to orgasm."

"You're so corny."

"The others didn't think so."

"What others?"

"The girls in my high school, when I did it last. Oh, Jesus!"

"Now what?"

Schwartz pulled the car over to the side and waited for the police car to come up and stop behind him.

"Serves you right, you show-off. Now don't fool around, and just let this poor policeman do his duty," she said, and squeezed his thigh so that he grimaced.

12

Until he saw the Volvo weave and buck and seem to be in trouble, Whelehan had stayed well behind. For a moment he wondered about staying out of sight, then he shook his head. It didn't matter. He could play it either way—both ways at once. He could stay in the open or do nothing or look on from a distance, and looking from a distance was turning out pretty nice what with this Karen taking to nude sunbathing. They were all bitches, all of them. Ball-breakers. Still, she was good-looking, this one, and probably knew a lot of the right people. He could arrest Schwartz for dangerous driving, give him a hard time . . . But, no, this was all his own turf, so why not play the nice guy? He turned on the siren and stepped on the gas.

"Inspector?"

"Ginger! Oh, Jesus. Hi. Sorry . . ." Schwartz shook his head and bit back a laugh.

Whelehan saw her kneading the side of Len's thigh. Didn't she think he could see? "I happened to see you pass as I was turning into this road. Then your car seemed to be in trouble, sort of surging forward and then slowing. Is everything all right?"

"Yes, yes. Absolutely. A damned yellow-jacket got

into the car. Drove us crazy until we stopped and got rid of it."

"Oh, good. Fine."

"Karen, this is Ginger Whelehan, Kitty and Tom's nephew. My wife, Karen Walker."

He looked into the car and put his arm across the wheel to shake her hand. Warm, like suntan oil on her belly. "How's everything going? You're in that terrific place on Sand Creek Way, aren't you?"

"Yes. It's very nice. My publisher's lent it to us."

He could see she still had her hand into Len's thigh. He'd like to grab a bit of hers. Len had a stupid smile on his face; must think he's blind and dumb as shit. "I haven't gotten around to reading that book of yours, you know, about Cézanne. But everyone says it's terrific."

"Well, thank you."

"I suppose you know the painters out here. I mean personally. Like de Kooning."

"No, I don't. I know the old Russian painters. We've just come—"

"Oh, yes. They're still around back in there. Well, don't want to keep you good people. Nice meeting you, Karen. Bye, Len. Take it easy."

"Bye, Ginger."

The Volvo disappeared around the bend. Who knows? Maybe he could get this Karen. Pretty, and how she rubbed that oil . . . There was that older woman in Sagaponic—well, not so old, really. But a painter. Wild, about forty. In their prime, know what it's all about. The husbands away in the city all week. Yes, maybe this Karen. Why not? They were all a little crazy in that world.

13

"**W**hat a coincidence." Karen laughed.

Schwartz laughed. "Coincidence, my ass. Still, what does it matter? And ain't *that* relaxed?"

"But what kind of a cop is this—do I know de Kooning?" asked Karen.

"A cop who's caught a dose of the Hamptons, or the Plimptons, my sweet."

When they parked by their high white fence, Karen said she was impressed with how much more relaxed—less crazy—he was. Laughing at being tailed was great progress.

"So there's hope?"

"More than hope—there's fettucini *vongole* and berry pie for dinner."

And there were mushrooms. Two hours later, as Schwartz set the table out by the pool, Karen answered the door and came out with the stunning Natasha. Schwartz remembered vodka and desire. Natasha was in a hurry, so she explained that the dish in her hands was even better heated up, but could she, because she was so starving and this was so wonderful?

So she took off the cover and offered it and when Karen and Schwartz hesitated she pulled slices of mushroom from the aromatic sauce and ate them, and when

Schwartz saw her licking her fingers he liked her a lot. Then Karen and he had slices of mushroom and they really were delicious and they had more and told Natasha she must stay for a drink, and Schwartz was glad the suggestion had come from Karen but he didn't want to think of why that might make him glad. But Natasha was off to dinner in Amagansett, so they never got to have the mushrooms heated because they just continued dipping in until they seemed to finish them with several gin and tonics and then came the fettucini *vongole*, green salad, and nice cold Californian wine and then hot blueberry and huckleberry pie with vanilla ice cream melting onto it and then coffee with some ludicrously arcane cognac they'd found in the house which they'd of course replace.

And then they watched some imbecilic TV and cuddled and were a bit drunk and very sleepy and just before they went to sleep Karen hugged Len and told him how proud she was that he really seemed to be getting the better of his uptightness or guilt or paranoia, or whatever.

He kissed her good night. "The whatever," he said. "That's what I'm proudest of."

14

Schwartz was so tired that he lay down full length in a hole in the ground. Faces appeared above him, looking down. There was old Kalubin, smiling, and beside him Anushka, with watery, steady blue eyes. Sasha and Piotr Glebor shook their heads at each other, looked down at him, and shook their heads again.

The light had to come from somewhere. Schwartz tried to see the sky over the faces, but he could see only the oak leaves and each needle of pine. Ginger Whelehan looked in to ask if everything was all right, now. Schwartz tried to answer but his jaw seemed far too heavy to move. Then Gallagher was there; thighs, belly, chest and chin a series of receding spheres to where his head leaned in, cheek to cheek against his nephew's.

A black and white beard moved across the light under two black, burning eyes. Vladimir Soloff nodded and said, "And after all, my friend, and after all, how much land does a man need?"

Schwartz knew the answer. Tears came to his eyes. His mouth, open to speak, filled with earth.

If only he could move. The earth on top of him was still not so heavy. But what was this? Just beside his head, if he turned it slightly, just there, down the wall of earth, level with his eye, a single red ant struggled furiously to drag a wasp. The yellow jacket, twenty times its size, was still alive, whirring and buzzing with rage as again and again the ant ran in, seized a furry leg in its mandible and tugged. The wasp curled its abdomen beneath its thorax, thrusting the great black lance of its sting.

Schwartz tried to call to the ant, to warn it, and found himself pinned under the barbed wire that covered the wasp's legs. The wasp was twenty times his size; he couldn't move under its weight. He tried to hold the sting back but his arms were weak and pinned to his chest. Then the thing ripped through into his stomach and he was screaming. Screaming but it wasn't his screaming. Screaming was her screaming.

He opened his eyes to look and it wasn't screaming. Karen was sitting on the side of the bed rocking forward and back groaning, "Len, Len, Len, Len, Len," and he knew the thing that ripped his stomach had ripped hers.

BOOK II

1

Their pain was the same, but only Karen was sweating. Her eyes weren't running like his. Schwartz helped her to the bathroom, telling her she had to vomit, they had to throw up everything. She couldn't stand straight; the pain pulled her down around her middle and she hugged herself, rocking, doubled over as she walked. She said she'd try, she'd be all right on her own now.

He encouraged himself in the other bathroom. He hated his fingers down his throat but knew he had to. Starting wasn't difficult; stopping was. How could there be more? It wasn't more—finally nothing came up but a terrific bitterness, a bile gas that burned his mouth. He washed his face, sipped water from his hands and went into the hall. His knees shook and he bumped into the walls.

He heard Karen over the rush of the water and behind the closed door, the long hoarse howl of empty retching. She was on her knees soaked with sweat, struggling to catch her breath between each shaking, sucked convulsion.

He put his hand to her forehead. It was too cold. Her hands slipped from the sides of the bowl and she slumped back.

"Wait, darling. Wait. Just lean against my legs,

here." He wet a towel and held it to her forehead. He
put a glass of water to her mouth.

"Drink it slowly. Drink. We're dehydrated from all
this." He thought that maybe he should put in salt.
They'd lost salt. Or sugar. Was it dextrose they needed?
They needed help.

He pulled Karen up so that she was propped between
him and the basin. He washed her.

Then he helped her into the bedroom and onto the
bed. They were shivering. He put a T-shirt on Karen
and one on himself. Hers said, "*nil illegitimus carbor-
undum est.*" It was stupid fake Latin but he wouldn't let
the bastards wear them down. He covered Karen with a
sheet and two blankets and felt as if he was going to
pass out, so he sat on the edge of the bed by the phone.
He had to focus. He knew the white brick on the floor
was a sneaker. He stared at it until it became almost
foot-shaped and then dialed 911 and said, "Poisoning,"
and within seconds a young man's voice came on.

"Suffolk County Hospital Emergency Service.
Name, address and telephone number, please."

"Leonard Schwartz, 6 Sand Creek Way, East Hampton. 537-5660."

"Thank you. What's the trouble?"

"I think my wife and I have food poisoning."

"From what?"

"Mushrooms or maybe clams."

"Have you been sick?"

"Yes."

"How long after eating was this?"

"I don't know. Eight, ten hours."

"Probably not bad clams. Bad clams sort of bounce
right back up."

"Oh."

"The mushrooms—were they ordinary store-bought?"

"No. They were . . . Wait. *Agaricus*. Yes, good wild mushrooms called 'abruptly bulbous *Agaricus*.'"

"*A-g-a-r-i-c-u-s*. Right. How are you feeling now?"

"Much better, but weak and cold."

"Stay warm. Drink some water with a bit of salt and sugar in it. You wouldn't happen to have any of the mushrooms or even any of what you threw up still around?"

"No. We finished the food and, call me unsentimental, but I didn't think to save any of the other."

"No need to be snide. It's just that it can be useful in identification. Still, you've vomited, and that's usually the best thing in these cases. Stay warm and don't panic. I'll check back with you in an hour or so. It sounds like you and your wife are probably all right now."

"Good. Thanks."

"I'll call back."

Schwartz hung up.

"What?" whispered Karen.

"We're probably all right. I'm going to get us some salty sweet water like the doctor said."

The doctor, at almost dawn? More likely a high school kid with a summer job. What did he expect, the chief gastrointestinal specialist of Mount Sinai to be sitting by the emergency phone in Riverhead on the off chance of telling Leonard Schwartz, who'd overeaten, that in his world-renowed opinion great wisdom had been shown in puking?

How sick can I be, thought Schwartz, if I can come up with foolishness like this? He supported Karen's head as she sipped the water.

"We're going to be fine, sweetheart," he said. "The

hospital will call back in an hour or so just to check up."

When at 8 A.M. the new shift at Suffolk Emergency telephoned the Schwartzes at East Hampton, the Schwartzes heard the ringing but couldn't move to the phone since that would mean leaving the toilets.

It wasn't funny, Schwartz thought, rocking. He'd call the hospital when he could, but it wasn't funny. He rocked. Earlier, he'd felt the bottom was falling out of his world; now the world was falling out of . . . It wasn't funny.

A few hours later when Schwartz called back, the voice on the phone noted the symptoms, asked how they felt, and when Schwartz answered they felt much better —tired but in very little pain—the voice suggested they keep up the drinking of water with just a bit of salt in it. They might call the hospital in the afternoon if anything changed.

Karen's hand was on his chest when he woke. She was smiling. "You were so good. You were as sick as I was and you took care of me and . . . Thank you, darling."

Schwartz brought tea and toast with honey. They were much better.

"Oh, I should call Soloff and Natasha and see if . . ."

"Yes."

But he felt too tired. Better, but too tired. Well, they'd sleep for a bit and when they woke . . .

He woke. It was still bright sunlight. Afternoon? Where was the sun? He looked at the clock. Nine in the morning? God! There was some pain. He turned. Karen was still asleep, breathing deeply, quietly, only the movement of the blanket . . . The light on her face gave her a deep golden tan, or not really golden so much as a yellow . . . A yellow . . .

Schwartz held up his hand. It was yellow. It wasn't in the light. He felt some pain, but it wasn't so bad.

"Karen?"

Karen opened her eyes and stared straight up. "Ouch," she said.

Schwartz dialed 911, asked for the hospital, got it, tried to say something and found himself crying. He put his hand over the phone. He'd pull himself together. He'd say it calmly. But he knew the end of a remission when he saw one.

Karen lay yellow, open-eyed, saying "Ouch" and "Ouch" very quietly.

He took his hand off the mouthpiece.

"Hello?" came the voice. "Please speak slowly. Hello?"

"This is Mr. Schwartz calling from East Hampton. Number 6 Sand Creek Way. The telephone number is 537-5660."

"Yes, right. Thank you. What's the problem?"

Keep calm, he thought, keep calm, and he said, "I think my wife and I are dying."

~~~~~~~ **2**

The same pain that kept Schwartz conscious through it all kept him oblivious. His last clear act had been a call to Gallagher, tellling him through sobs of pain and panic and grief that they'd been poisoned and that he was watching Karen turn yellow-gray and die.

So he wasn't sure if it was an ambulance or a heli-
copter, Riverhead or Manhattan. Whatever it was, it
took a week to wake up to, though he knew he hadn't
been asleep. That pain shredded him inside from chest
to groin; that pain kept grinding under the drugs, the
drips and, finally, dialysis.

"Where? Where's Karen? Is Karen here? Where's
Karen?" He was going to start crying.

A hand touched his shoulder. A big man in light blue
leaned in over him.

"It's okay, Lenny. Karen's okay, pal. She's pulling
through fine. She's just fine. It's you we were worried
about. You've been giving us a hard time."

It was Gallagher. Schwartz felt the tears roll down
his face. Karen was all right. Here was Gallagher.
Where?

"Where is this?"

"Mount Sinai. I was damned if I'd let them take you
two any place but the best. We got a state police chop-
per to bring you right into the city. You two have had
the best G-I and toxicology people in the world fixing
your guts. Oh, jeeze, Lenny, there I go with my big
dumb mouth. Sorry, buddy."

Gallagher was shaking his head, but "fixing your
guts" was fine with Schwartz. He felt better. They certainly did their best, the Department. They pulled you to
pieces, but they certainly used super glue to stick you
together again. What pieces?

"What happened, Tom?"

"You two ate some of the world's nastiest stuff, and
those jerks at Emergency out there were too lazy or
something to check it out. Seems they only knew about

the good mushrooms you ate. That right? What the hell happened?"

"Oh, Jesus. It's all coming back. That girl—Natasha. Soloff. Were there any other . . . Where's Karen? I want to see Karen, Tom."

"She's right down the hall. I'll get her to come over."

"Tom, were there any others poisoned?"

"Not that we know. And we checked, because we didn't know if you ate at a party or a restaurant or home."

"I thought we just had too many, but I thought they were good mushrooms. I thought . . . Jesus! It could have . . . He could have! I mean, it's unprovable. The only risk he would have run was that it mightn't kill me. No, but if he was also sick? Oh . . ."

"Calm down, Lenny. Take it easy. You saying someone purposely . . . Oh, Jesus. I don't believe you, but now you've got me going. You saying it was connected with that business out there?"

Schwartz nodded.

"Shit, I don't think so. But let's call it a day with that. You give me the nod, what you have on it, and we'll see if we can at least get a formal investigation going, right up at state level. I promise you."

Schwartz tried to think about it, but nothing would stay in his mind. He nodded. "But this isn't the nod. Not yet. I'll talk to you later. Tom, thanks. I mean for Karen, for getting us here . . ." He felt tears coming again. What was wrong with him?

And then Gallagher was bending over him, patting his shoulder, trying to be delicate with his big mitts.

"Take care, Lenny."

Schwartz shut his eyes, touched.

* * *

"Touched! The bastard gets me into all this, almost gets you killed, and when he pats me I'm touched! I must be touched in the head." Schwartz tread water, talking to Karen two weeks later at the end of July, at the deep end of the pool.

She pushed some wet hair back of her ear. "You know I'm not exactly Tom Gallagher's champion, but don't put the blame on him. You took this on; he didn't force you. And it's you who still refuses to tell him 'enough,' set up the formal investigation so you can gracefully retire into what's left of your liver and our summer. And isn't a formal investigation the whole idea?"

"Yes. No. No, the investigation would get, maybe, maybe with great luck, one crooked cop. But those pro- cesses are so bureaucratically muscle-bound that they'd have to miss all the other four hundred and twelve very bad things going on. Karen?"

Karen had pushed away from the edge and swam a slow crawl to the other end and back.

"All right, so given my particular background I have to go hard for a crooked cop. Guilt, expiation, an athe- ist's purgatory. But give me a break."

She blew water from her mouth. "A break? I was damned sick, but you almost died. A break? I don't like to watch you nearly die for some private, pigheaded, guilty . . . Oh, God. And I can't keep watching you. I have to go back to the city for research, and I have to go out to Baldock Island. You know that and you're still thinking of continuing to snoop and stir things? Jesus, no! No, I couldn't go through that again. I'm not going to. Len?"

Schwartz lay on his back and floated halfway down the pool. The sky was bright blue. Paradise azure. He turned and did his own slow crawl back. Swimming was good. It was getting him well again.

"But it's you," he said. "You're the one who insisted we come back out here. You're the one who has to do her job so much that she's convinced herself the poisoning was accidental."

"But Natasha wasn't ill."

"So she says. Anyway, she only had a few pieces and they could have been only the good ones. She could have known, somehow. It only needed one or two slices of that lovely destroying angel at the bottom to get us."

Karen held the pool lip and kicked. "Oh, that's still painful. But Soloff was poisoned too. Not like we were, but pretty badly. How do you explain that? I mean, I know you will, but I'm curious about your paranoid twist."

"Karen, you're arguing against yourself. First you say it's my investigation that nearly killed me, and now you say it was only an unfortunate accident. As for Soloff—wasn't it convenient that he was at friends' in Connecticut with a convenient doctor present and then a convenient home cure. So there's no record, unless I find that doctor and squeeze the truth from him. But there is no doctor. Soloff's lying. That's my explanation. It's what happened."

"And I thought you were more relaxed. You really are getting crazy again."

"I never should have stopped. I stopped, I relaxed, and the real trouble started. Okay, I'll tell you. Let's call it a draw for now. You get on with your research. You go out to that island where Count Vlad the poisoner sponges off the rich, and I'll just go on being a little crazy and wary so maybe both of us will survive this vacation. Jake had it right."

"What? What right?"

"At Mount Sinai. Remember? He hugged us and said how sorry and scared he'd felt. And then he looked out over the park and said we were both jerks."

"He did. My darling son. Only it was Madison and you couldn't see out. We got good care from your boss, but it didn't run to the park side of the hospital. Remember?"

"Quibbler," Schwartz said, and decided that he needed his arms around Karen.

She pulled him under the water and kissed him; they came up hugging.

"Mmm," she said. "You feeling better."

"You mean feeling you better?"

"That too. Is it the long nap you took this morning?" In his pause she pushed away. "Oh, you didn't? Don't fib. I caught you. What did you do when I was out?"

"I just sat and read."

"What?"

"Land records, stuff like that."

"We don't have stuff like that."

"No. Over at the county offices in Riverhead. And I talked with some people too. Interesting." He smiled at Karen's glare. "But interesting in a relaxing way."

"I hate you, Len." She splashed water in his face.

"Listen, there are lots of folk around here worthier of your hate. Want to hate? I'll bet you find a few hate-ables tomorrow night."

"At Rita Troost's dinner party? Oh, Len. I like her. Please, no scenes. Please."

"I like Rita too. And aren't I always nice? Did *I* put poison in our hors d'oeuvres or was it your passionate and lovely Leo Tolstoy?"

"You're angry because you feel guilty that I was . . . that I got sick."

"Darling," he said, "you're damned right."

As they pulled close he had the feeling they were being watched, professionally observed. He'd worried Karen enough; besides, he knew he'd see nothing if he turned to look, so he shut his eyes and licked the water from her cool, soft cheek.

3

Schwartz was following the others in when Phil Troost put a hand on his jacket and smiled.

"Lenny, ah, I hope you'll . . . There's a . . . Well, this is a stuffy old place, but men are supposed to wear jacket *and* necktie to dinner."

Phil had blond curly hair and a blond curly smile and was older than he looked and charmingly embarrassed for Schwartz. Phil wore a pale yellow necktie covered with small, well-ordered rows of red sperm. This was a necktie Schwartz recognized as appearing every spring in the city, in droves. Not droves, though the men wore them like sheep, but in huge flocks, like starlings. Schwartz was nodding. Like starlings because they were birdbrained, though more like locusts, because they plagued. . . .

Schwartz was nodding and saying, "Oh, of course,"

as the maître d' ducked into a doorway and out again
with five or six neckties in his hand.

Four of the neckties looked decently bland, the fifth
was louder but within the pale and Schwartz chose the
sixth. The sixth had obviously been left behind by the Bad
Taste Club of Sasketoon when they'd wandered in here
during the early 1970s at the height, or width, of the wide
wide ties. They hadn't, of course, penetrated farther than
the vestibule of the Southampton Dining Club.

Phil plucked up his smile as Schwartz decided on a
three inch Windsor knot to complement the six inch
wide apex, or was it vortex or nadir, above his belt. He
checked the mirror. Perfect: the plastic shine of heavy
manmade fiber, the interlocking one inch diamonds of
alternating baby blue, bright green and brilliant brown.

"May I, Lenny, just fix . . . It seems your collar's but-
toned down *under* the tie, actually."

"Oh, thanks, Phil. That's fine."

And then the entrance—not a jaw dropper, but
something of a head turner. And such heads. A few
younger, but basically the heads with hair were curly
blue (white women), wavy white (white men) and curly
white (black men). And the curly white-haired men
were not seated at the tables, not a one.

Karen, mistress of decorum, rolled her eyes only
slightly on seeing the tie as she stood waiting with Rita
Troost and Phil's wife, Patsy, and Lulu and Charles
something-or-other, Rita's friends, so that the ladies
could be seated first. They could have been seated first
before, but this way all the gentlemen could observe
them being seated first. Ah, mores, ah, temper, temper,
now, thought Schwartz, who was seated between Rita
and Lulu.

He turned to Lulu's question. "No, I drink, but I

can't for some time. Karen and I recently had a spot of liver trouble."

"Liver spots? Poor things. We have good friends with bad livers. Bob and Sybil Hereford, the Earl and Countess of Hereford. You know them?"

"No."

"What's that? I'm a bit deaf."

"No."

"Oh. They've spent the summers here for years. Do you and your wife?"

"No, we seem to stay around Park Slope most summers."

"Park where? Tuxedo Park?"

"No. Park Slope."

"Oh, Brooklyn! Brooklyn, you might not believe, but Brooklyn used to be so...I remember as a girl going over and riding ponies with Barbara Delancey. They had acres and acres of gardens and such a lovely ...Do you know the Delanceys?"

"No, I—"

"Mostly dead now."

She went back to sipping her martini, holding the glass with fingers twisted in arthritis, encrusted in sapphire and diamond. Lulu in profile looked hard and selfish and arrogant. But, Schwartz noted, when she turned full face she didn't look as nice. Still, he'd try. He'd promised Karen.

"And where do you live in the winter?" he asked.

"Charles and I live in Durban."

"Durban?"

"What?"

"Durban?"

"Yes. South Africa. A very beautiful and very misunderstood place."

Schwartz considered. He considered he'd done his best and the hell with Lulu back in town. He'd . . . He'd . . . He excused himself from the table.

He looked into the men's room mirror; the cold water ran down his face. Behind that were shadows, one of them his dead father's.

Funny place, huh, Dad? he said to himself.

The shadow shook its head; his father's once bright angry features were somber.

Dad, I have to spend time with these—

"Lackey."

No. It's not—simple, anymore.

"Lackey."

There's a chance I can get land back for the Indians out here, so—

"To sit in such a place with such people and enjoy disliking it? A lackey's pleasure." And the shadow turned back into the wall.

Schwartz looked down. The tie was soaked. Good.

"Are you all right?"

It was bright, bouncy Phil.

Schwartz nodded and wiped his face. "Yes, just a little weak. I've been ill."

"Yes, that must have been horrible, mushroom poisoning."

"Where'd you hear that?"

Phil came up to the mirror and peered at his face. "Karen was telling us before dinner. Awful. Oh, and I think my mother had heard it from her earlier."

"I thought maybe Vladimir would have told you."

"Vladimir?"

"Vladimir Soloff. I'm sure you know him."

Phil came away from the mirror. "Yes, I've had the honor. I think at some art shows in New York and out here. A great painter, and I think a great man—what he went through for freedom in the U.S.S.R."

"Yes," Schwartz said, stepping between Phil and the door, "he went through a lot. I don't know if it was for freedom, though. So that's how you know him?"

"Yes."

"Phil . . . Phil. How can I put this? Just because I clown around behind this necktie doesn't mean I'm stupid. I've been out to County Records. Soloff represented a group interested in changing the zoning of the Russian Art Community land. You know, that cozy bit of land? You should. You chaired the zoning board that granted it. As a matter of fact, you prepared quite an elegant argument in favor of two-acre-lot development and pushed it through. Remember?"

"Oh, sure, the Russian place. I do a lot of that, so I can't always remember—"

Schwartz put his finger lightly into the middle of Phil's tie. "Phil, please don't give me any shit about not remembering. Don't bother telling me how two-acre-lot zoning represents minimum development density. You used that clever, curly Wall Street head of yours to turn around half a dozen forest conservation laws and precedents."

"Hey, wait a second, dinner guest. If you're accusing me of believing in free enterprise, I'm guilty and damned proud of it."

Phil backed away. Schwartz moved with him so that his finger remained on Phil's tie. "Not free enterprise. Fixed enterprise. For one thing, the people Soloff represented weren't even clear owners."

"I remember they had power of attorney, so representation—"

Schwartz's hand went lightly around Phil's tie.

"Coming back to you, is it? Good. Look, Phil, land scams aren't my line of work. But maybe you'll remember other things? Not now, of course. How gauche of me, your guest here at the Martin Bormann Supper Club."

"Really, Lenny, let's not get—"

"Let's? Let's? What's this *us* business? Isn't the message clear? I'm after your ass, old beach boy. My business is homicide and I think you're up to your neck in the Amboys murder."

"What?"

Troost looked down. Behind the tie, Schwartz's first and second fingers had moved up to and either side of Phil's windpipe. They stayed there, very lightly.

"You think you're scaring me?"

"I certainly hope so, Phil. I think you're in this so deep, you're slipping right under the sand. And if I scare you into cooperating with me, I think we can save your neck. Now I'm not saying you did it. I don't think you're strong enough to have bashed a head in like that. Terrible."

"But I only know how the body was found!"

"And if you don't cooperate, maybe I'll hint to Whelehan that you *are* cooperating. And Whelehan—you remember Whelehan, don't you, Phil? The young police detective who answered your call so promptly when your poor mother dug Amboys from the dunes? No? The redheaded cop on the make who's going to graft his way into places like this with the likes of you and Lulu the lulu?"

Pushing with his first and second fingers, Schwartz had moved Phil so that his back was to the door. "And if Whelehan thinks you're cooperating with me, well . . . You may have your doubts about *my* toughness, but you ought to know how tough *that* bad cop is."

Phil's hand moved up toward Schwartz's fingers. Schwartz stared at it and Phil's hand dropped back. Then Schwartz dropped his own hand.

"Well, Phil, let's not be rude and keep the ladies waiting."

"Inspector Schwartz, I think you must be a little bit crazy."

"That's right. Just keep that in mind." Schwartz held open the door. "Oh, and Phil . . ."

"What?"

"Is my necktie straight?"

~~~~~~~ **4**

Karen had gone back to New York for the week to do research; she'd spoken of the sticky atmosphere with the Russians since the poisoning. Schwartz had understood that to also mean the sticky atmosphere with him. On the phone, he told her, of Soloff's sorrow, wondering if she'd understand that to also mean the relief he felt being on his own. He was saying how sorry Soloff was being by note, by phone call, by a pound of fresh beluga caviar delivered by motorcycle express. He'd asked the messenger if an antidote had been dispatched with the gift.

Karen thought that in questionable taste. Schwartz said questionable taste was just the point.

Still, the fellow was begging forgiveness. Over the top and, besides, not even Russian.

"What?" asked Karen.

"Forgiveness. Tolstoy, somewhere, has a fallen woman beg for understanding, not forgiveness."

"It was Dostoyevsky, not Tolstoy. A fallen man, not a woman. In a tavern in *Crime and Punishment*. His name was Marmeladov, and why not ask Vladimir over for lunch? It could help both of us—all the Russians are so embarrassed. You know it would be easier without me there."

"Karen, you're right. I will, and I've decided to forgive you for being too smart for me to understand."

"You're really angry, aren't you? Don't answer, Len, think about it. I should be back on Saturday, if all this MOMA research goes well. Stay out of trouble. Love you."

He loved her and put the phone down and picked it up and tomorrow for lunch was fine with Soloff.

"After all," he said, showing the tall man in, "you suffered, too, for those mistaken mushrooms."

"Ah, but not so badly, my kind friend, as you and your wife."

Soloff was a sensational figure in his prophet's beard and paint-splattered blue and white striped shirt and long, loose linen pants. He stood with his hands behind his back, rocking slightly, taking in everything without appearing to shift his eyes from his host.

"Leonard, my friend, I can only think that I became too confident, that I took some *virosa* without digging up the base for identification. And then, with Karen and you eating so much . . . And you know how subjective poisoning is. It appears that Natasha and I are less affected than Karen. And as for you, my poor fellow . . . I cannot forgive myself."

"Oh, go on, Vladimir, do it—forgive yourself. I'm reduced to soft drinks for a few months, but, after all, I'm not reduced to nothing."

He handed Soloff the vodka on the rocks and sipped his iced tea. "I know what you mean about things affecting people differently. There used to be something I wasn't allergic to—the other kids were. I forget. Anyhow, let's stop all this talk about poison and have a nice simple lunch. What do you think of Bob's collection?" Schwartz waved his hand out to the walls.

"Well, these are very knowing painters. Clever in color and form and line. Technically excellent. But I am sorry to say that mostly they cannot transcend their banal subjects *or* their brilliant renderings because this work is trapped in that American disease of materialism, a total and dangerous materialism. Ha! You see? I'm not such a blind worshiper of everything American," Soloff said, bouncing on his toes as if about to execute a *jeté* or spring at Schwartz's throat. Instead, he bent his head in a mock bow.

And so through lunch they spoke of painting and materialism and of the difference between receiving a large amount of money for a work and working for a large amount of money. Schwartz decided not to bring up Whelehan; he'd keep everything in a nice low key. Then they spoke of how much they liked the old Kalubins and Glebors, people and paintings. And Vladimir said that he'd acted for the children and grandchildren only because they had come to him knowing of his patrons and their powerful contacts, fearing that the old folk in their

naïveté would be swindled. And so he had helped, done
what he could. Nothing more.

Schwartz nodded, smiled, cleared up and suggested a
stroll.

"Yes, yes, very nice here," said Soloff as they started
down the lane outside the fence. "Perhaps you see how
woods and houses can go together."

They walked past pines and scrub oak. Schwartz
pointed out how fifteen or fifty or ninety feet back and
to each side were houses and houses and houses. "So
that it's not," he said, "real woods. It's the remnants of
real woods—cheap landscaping."

Soloff said they were nice homes and people needed
homes, surely, decent homes rather than those boxes
provided by the state in places like the benighted Soviet
Union. Schwartz said no doubt, but did people really
need to destroy the few woods left out here for nice *fifth*
homes, especially when many other people in this en-
lightened country had no more than boxes? And didn't
Vladimir see the contradictory logic of his stance?

Vladimir did not. He told his friend Schwartz that
this was to make assumptions.

His friend Schwartz said assumptions? Assumptions?
The Russian land was now zoned for two-acre, single
family lots. That meant at least four hundred thousand
dollars each. And that was no assumption. Just how
totally ignorant did his friend Vladimir think he was?

Friend Vladimir muttered, "No more than most lib-
erals."

Schwartz said he'd heard that and clearly Vladimir
was not ignorant, was, in fact, smart enough to understand who those woods really belonged to.

Soloff had stopped where the lane ended in a circle, a

patch of scrub undergrowth sloping down behind him to a small red-brown pond. "And who would that be?"

"The Shinnecock Indians."

"Ah, yes. This land was once theirs, so of course you think—"

"No, not just in that sense. Real, owned, deeded land."

"So old Kalubin and the Glebors—"

"Not them. Taken from the Indians before that and sold later to the Russians, who bought it in good faith. And then, recently, the stolen deeds traced, and then the tracer, who was too honest to be bribed silent, had to be kept silent with his head bashed in on the beach, and the coroner's report shows it would have taken a very strong, very tall person to do that particular damage."

Soloff narrowed his eyes, bounced on his toes and said, "I am not stupid, as you say, my friend. I say that if anyone but a police officer had so insulted me, I would act accordingly. But, as you are the law, and as I very much respect your wife—"

"We can leave Karen out of this. And the law. I'm in jeans and T-shirt. No badge, no gun. So get it all off your chest."

Schwartz tensed, waiting for Soloff to leap or come in swinging. Instead, he was coming toward him with open arms and tears in his eyes.

"My friend," he said. And before Schwartz knew it, Soloff was hugging him.

Jesus, what a crazy sentimental Russian. Maybe he'd had him all wrong. Maybe . . . Hold it. A hug was a hug, but this . . .

"Okay, okay," he said, heaving, trying to push Soloff away. But the big hands were locked into the small of

his back, pulling so that his chest was crushed against
the blue and white shirt. Arms like steel bands pressed
into his ribs, squeezing out the air.... Air! Jesus, no
breath left, passing out ...

Schwartz's right knee came up between the tall man's
spread legs. Soloff's eyes closed with pain, his arms
loosened. Schwartz sucked in air and shoved his palm
hard into Soloff's chin.

He fell backward, still clasping Schwartz in the
weakened bear hug, and they fell down the slope behind, rolling over and over in the green tangled undergrowth.

Schwartz was screaming, "I am so mad!" as he saw it
and grabbed fistfuls and rubbed it into what showed of
Soloff's face over the beard.

The green shiny flailing was over in seconds.
Schwartz stood up. Soloff rolled back and forth on the
ground clutching at his face.

"Oh, yes, that's what it was," said Schwartz. "Poison
ivy. Never affects me. Subjective, isn't it? Sorry. You
know, that day and a half when I watched Karen so
sick ... And you such a good mycologist. Well, I suppose that's gotten the poison out of my system. Forgive
... I mean, you understand?"

Soloff stood up sobbing; he put his hands out to see.
His eyes, swollen shut, were two fat fists stuck into the
sockets. His face was a mass of white blisters against
bright red. It looked like a mushroom—a gigantic fly
agaric. But it certainly wasn't funny. The man was hor-
ribly allergic. He'd have to be taken to a hospital right
away.

Schwartz led the stumbler by his ulcerated hand and
tried very hard to stop smiling.

5

Soloff lies in the guest room at Alexei Kalubin's house feeling drowsy from the histamine injections.

Well, well, so the little yid policeman had turned vicious.

He is in pain, but it is already better knowing it won't last. What is a day's pain, a week's, to one who has suffered year after year? He will wake without pain, and then . . . And then . . . The pain is a Sign, a Blessing.

So, so, so. This Schwartz is strong and clever. But we shall see, little man. How strong? How clever? Can he imagine that a little rash will make Vladimir Soloff panic?

Tell Whelehan? No. He would do something too crude, too obvious. Natasha. So. First, sleep. Sleep, then speak with Natasha. Sleep.

His beautiful Natasha will know what to do.

6

Natasha had to speak with him. Yes, she'd spoken with Vladimir this morning and he was much better. What he'd done to Vladimir was wrong, though she could understand his anger. But it wasn't about that foolishness. It was about the land.

He pursed his lips and pulled his jaw down in a sort of baboon howl, drawing the razor up the side of his chin past his mouth. Did the skin actually tighten and make the shaving easier, or was that just habit? Or trying to distract himself from thinking he was thinking about Natasha coming over and Karen in New York. The important thing was not to think "I'm not like that." That would be the depth of self-deception. But he wasn't. Deceiving himself? No, wasn't like that.

He washed off the shaving soap and brushed his hair. Well, was he supposed to meet *anyone* with shaving lather on his face and his hair over his eyes? And there was nothing ominous in choosing this Hawaiian shirt, in checking to see how many undone buttons would show the hair on his chest.... His chest didn't look yellow anymore. Many times he'd fool around like this getting dressed. Yes. The white jeans were clean and so were his bare feet. There, now. Natasha wasn't taller, or maybe if she wore heels would be, but just a bit? No, certainly not. In heels she'd be as tall as he was without them. Without heels? Calmly, Leonard. Calmly. This would have to be better than yesterday with Soloff. A disaster would be better than yesterday with Soloff. The business at hand. Here were drinks, ice. Music: what to play?

Something Russian, of course. *Boris Godunov*? A bit too intense. Yes, the Tchaikers; nothing like some *Romeo and Juliet*. Nothing so corny. A Borodin quartet? No, something modern. Stravinsky? But restrained, no rites. Neoclassical Stravers? No, too cool. Oh, screw it. A little Johnnie Griffin would do fine.

Okay, okay. Where the hell is she? Who cares. I have plenty to do without getting excited every time an incredibly beautiful young woman with whom I think I may have exchanged meaningful glances just before she may have poisoned me happens to drop by.

He sat on one of the white sofas, put his feet up and was immediately back to the night when Natasha had come by, except in this version Karen wasn't there. He held Natasha by the pool, their clothes dropped off, they dropped into the water, rolling voluptuously in the steaming . . . Doorbell!

Doorbell. All right. Just walk slowly. You'll get there.

When he opened the door she was so much prettier than in his daydream that he was sure he gawked or gaped or gasped like some acned jughead until he said a brilliant. "Hi, come on in," after which he was sure she'd heard his gulp.

They went out to the swimming pool. Drinks on the table? Yes. Water in the pool? Yes, yes. Would

she like to drop her clothing. "Would you like a drop
to drink?"

"No, thank you, Inspector."

"No, thank you, not Inspector. Len."

They sat at the table. Her eyes were large and black;
her hair was honey brown; her legs were . . .

"Driving over here I tried to think of what I'd say,
how I'd begin. And I found myself getting very angry. I
feel I've been put in an impossible situation between
Vladimir, you, my grandparents, and . . . Oh, I'm . . . I
think I would like a drink. Gin and tonic, please."

He made the drink and took club soda for himself.
He was content to sip in silence and look at her eyes,
her hair, her legs which . . .

"Why don't you say something? Ask me some questions? Cross-examine me. Is that what it is?"

"Sometimes silence is a technique for getting you to
talk. Or maybe I'm tongue-tied."

"Look, there's already a great deal of strain between
those who want the property developed and those who
don't."

"And where are you in that?"

"In the middle. I've tried to remain neutral. Maybe,
after my grandparents and the Glebors are—are gone,
some of it could be developed so the family could get
some money, and the rest could be . . . Oh, I don't know,
a nature reserve or county or state park. But my personal views aren't so important. It's Valodya."

"Valodya?"

"That's what we call Vladimir. I have to explain.
First, please, please, please believe that he didn't poison
you or me or himself intentionally."

"That's a lot to ask, but you ask it very nicely."
Schwartz was looking at his toes, thinking of how Nata-

sha hadn't mentioned Karen among those stricken. "Suppose I say okay, I'll try to believe that. Then what?"

"Well, first there's Vladimir himself. I mean as a painter. You realize, don't you, that he's the first major, original painter to emerge from the Soviet Union since the late twenties. A miracle, a double miracle in that he was well known in the West. That helped save him. So he's not merely another defected dancer or dissident writer or physicist. He's unique."

Schwartz smiled. "I'll give him that." He heard Griffin. Griffin was groovin'.

"Perhaps you wouldn't be so sarcastic if you knew how he's revitalized our art community. There are no artists in my parents' generation. The usual rebellion against their artist parents, I suppose. They're all very standard home and business types. But among the grandchildren, some of us, like me, are painters. We're not close, though, and we never really thought much about the place out here and what our Russianness meant. Until Valodya. He's come and taught us, and he's a great teacher of painting, so good that he doesn't seem to be teaching. Even the controversy he's brought has been good. Very good and exciting; the old folks haven't been so happy in years. And more—when you know him you find he has a great power and a great gentleness, a—humility."

"I know. I've eaten some of his humble pie."

Natasha glared. She stood and walked to the pool and turned back and stood next to the table. A wonderful smell . . .

"I don't find that funny. I don't find you funny. No, oh, that's not so, either. That first time, at that family dinner, you were funny. Very charming, something crazy and attractive about you, if you want to know."

"I do, I do," he said.

"Why are you being so—aggressive? I mean, if you think Vladimir's guilty of some crime, just charge him. Do it. But all this innuendo and harassment. It's horrible, your calling him a swindler and a thief and worse."

"Hey, I haven't called him anything—except weird and uncooperative. Both are true. On the other hand, neither is illegal."

Natasha's hand was tight and white-knuckled around her glass. He saw a tremor run up her tanned forearm. He thought he'd like to run up with it.

"Len, Valodya is very dear to me and to the others. However strange he seems to you, he's acted well for us, even for those who find his plans for the Community of Real Russia sort of silly and juvenile. He's important. And this business with you not only shakes his confidence but shakes ours. The man has been through so much. It's . . . Oh, I can't explain"

"Yes you can. You're doing pretty well. And I can understand, though I've never gone in for gurus myself. You also sound a little in love."

Natasha put her glass down. She smiled and ran her hands through her hair. Her lips were full and her nose was long and snub at its end, the nice mix, Schwartz imagined, of her Jewish-Slavic grandparents.

"Oh, yes," she said, "a little in love. We had an affair last year but it wasn't . . . It didn't work: we couldn't work, couldn't paint well and figured out it was a sign and became friends. That's what we are now —loving friends. Not lovers. And you? Are you a little jealous?"

Was he? He got up and walked past her to the edge of the pool. Under the hot wind its surface ripple fell across the bottom in small S's of light and shadow. Lines, sinuous, sensual.

"Yes," he said, still looking down, thinking that was what made him such a bad cop, then thinking that he should first have thought that was what made him such a bad husband, then thinking nothing at all but listening to Natasha's footsteps and watching her shadow drop across his bare feet.

"I thought so," she said. "At first, at that dinner, I didn't think you even noticed me, and I'm used to being noticed and I didn't like that. But when I came over here that night with . . . When I dropped in, I noticed how you looked at me."

"Licking your fingers," he said, looking up. But that, he knew, was also licking poison.

She stood very close to him. "Why were you looking at me like that?"

"I think I'm interested in appetites."

"Part of your work?"

"Part of my appetites."

The wind dropped. The sounds blew down and soared up out of Johnny Griffin's tenor. He heard her breathe. Her smell was light sandalwood and a honey sweat.

"And how," she asked, "is your appetite now?"

"I'm very hungry," he said, moving into her breath and sandalwood and honey. He felt where that tremor had run to and where it was going.

"Tell me something, something strange and arcane, Leonard. Leonard the lion."

Natasha was stroking his cheek. His neck lay across the top of her thigh, the back of his head on her belly. He turned and kissed the thick dark honey

of her hair, kissed into the sandalwood damp under
the flesh of her thigh.

"Natasha, you are so beautiful."

"You're beautiful, too, Leonard. You have a big,
beautiful—appetite." She laughed. "But won't you tell
me something strange?"

Griffin blew a creamy obbligato.

He said, "Let me think." He kissed his way up the
curve of her stomach and licked her belly button and
kissed where the ribs began and skin was lighter and up
and over her breast until he lay half on her, half at her
side. Both of them were covered with sweat and soon
they'd swim, and it was all right because it was so
purely physical. And it wasn't, of course; nothing so
physically good remained just physical.

"Here's something," he said. "We were talking about
gurus. Do you know the origin of the word 'guru'?"

"No. Tell me."

"It goes back to Sanskrit, where it means 'heavy' or
'serious.'"

"Yes, my beautiful lion man. That's arcane but not
strange."

"Ah, but that same word's at the root of our word 'to
grieve.'"

She put her hand under his chin and turned his face
so that she looked into his eyes. Her look was concen-
trated by some pain or anger. "Leonard, is that true?"

Griffin was into a breathy blues.

"Yes," he said. "It's too clever for me to make up,
the link between guru and grief."

7

Why hadn't he been told? He knew her, one of Soloff's Russian groupies from the art community. Had
she been sent? Was Vladimir keeping something from
him? Silly man.

Whelehan adjusted his legs.

Well, this was fine. Detective Inspector Schwartzie
had an overrated reputation. Very dumb, groping by the
pool like that. And he'd gotten a great shot—only a few
seconds, but he had the smart-ass cop and the Russian
bitch naked together as they closed the curtains. Yeah, it
would do nicely. And the same background as in the
video with Karen. How would he use them? He wasn't
sure, but the videos were great. A good cop always had
a backup.

He moved carefully in the tree blind.

8

It was wonderful; Schwartz felt terrible. Dreams, day-dreams, what had he done? He knew. Twenty years of flirting and he assumed he'd never . . . Always knew one day . . . What had he done to Karen? Ah, what was the harm. Natasha was a beautiful free spirit. He'd called Brooklyn that morning to confess, but Karen wasn't in —out early or could have spent the night in Manhattan. Hearing the phone ring and the ring unanswered, he'd been relieved. A sign.

He'd gone into Southampton to cheer himself up by buying a shirt and was standing in front of all the summer stripes at the Saks shirt counter before remembering that shopping for clothes depressed him. The pins, the plastic bits around the collars, cold tape on his neck and poky dressing rooms where his trousers spilled change onto a carpet of lint.

He walked around. The wide brick sidewalks seemed full of heavy children eating ice-cream cones. The ice cream dripped down wrappers printed with red and yellow words in Scandinavian.

He felt awful. There was a bookshop. It was like after he'd taken the cocaine bribe. A headache, a guilty pounding in the ears. It looked like a good bookshop. He had betrayed Karen. Betrayed. A woman came out of the bookshop. She stopped and stared at him. Why hadn't he left well enough . . . Why didn't everyone leave everyone else alone?

The woman walked up to him. "Your wife is so good!"

Schwartz felt giddy. "What? Who . . . How did you know?"

"Karen Walker? That book of hers is so marvelous. We met in the city last year? Nina Roberts? Mr. Walker, I remember you're a . . ."

"Bookbinder," he said, going toward the door. "Walker the bookfinder, the bookmaker," he continued, for no reason other than to keep from saying "Student, Raskalnikov the student."

Ten minutes later he'd calmed down in the book smells and quiet of the store. He held a pamphlet, wondering why he hadn't come here before. What kind of a cop was he? He warned himself not to answer: it was a trick question. He'd skimmed books by Amboys at the library, but here were others. He looked at the pamphlet's title page again, went to the office door at the back and knocked.

"In."

"Hi. Excuse me. Did you publish this?"

The rock faced man at the desk looked over his half glasses. "Yup. Interested in local windmills?"

"No. Amboys."

"Police?"

"Yup."

"Proof?"

"Yup." Schwartz went to the desk and showed him. "Len Schwartz."

"Richard Cooke. Pull up a chair."

"Thanks." Schwartz sat down near the desk. Sit,

stand, up, down, sure, thanks, please. Why the hell was he a policeman? Why were Natasha's thighs so wonderful? The way her hair . . .

Cooke cleared his throat. "You wanted to know. . ."

"What? Oh, sorry. Yes. Anything."

"I've published six or seven of Victor's monographs and two of his books in conjunction with the local historical society of which I'm currently president."

"Were you a friend?"

"Sure. Knew Victor for . . . Must have been fifty years."

"He ever mention discovering a lost land deed belonging to the Shinnecocks?"

"Nope. Wait, let me think. Nope. Nothing like that."

Schwartz sighed. It was a nice old room full of books and papers and file cabinets bulged open and photos of writers. Steinbeck, Capote . . . Why was he a cop? If he had a bookstore, none of this—

Another cough.

"Sorry, Mr. Cooke. I'm getting depressed. It seems no one knows anything. You say you knew Victor Amboys all that time, yet he never confided."

"Well, yes. But we were more friends in sharing an interest in local history and books. He wasn't someone who'd discuss anything he'd found that wasn't researched, documented or somehow proven to his standards. And they were pretty high."

"Yes, that's what Chief Sun Johnson said."

The crags of Cooke's face softened. He smiled. "Isn't Sun Johnson a terrific old guy?"

Schwartz nodded and smiled back. Here was the first local white who—

"It's too damned bad about that grandson. He's simpleminded, you know."

Schwartz nodded.

"Wait. Victor did have a close friend—Jansen, the hatmaker, over in Hampton Bays. They're old. I haven't seen them for years. But still alive. Why don't you try them? I'll get their address." He looked through a card file, wrote and handed the slip of paper to Schwartz.

"Thanks."

"Sure. Oh, Inspector, I've heard about... Well, I guess I know a lot of people around here and I've heard about some of the... of your... I'm trying to say that not all of us around here are racists and snobs."

"Thanks."

"About the Jansens," Cooke said, sliding his glasses back up his nose and looking down at his desk, "they're not what they may seem."

Schwartz thought of that, driving west out of town. Then he passed the pathetic concrete wigwam "trading post" for the pathetic reservation, and he promised himself that he'd try to... And then there was the bay and the ocean gleaming to his left as he took the curves on the Shinnecock Hills. And ninety miles straight ahead was Karen, betrayed. He had betrayed her.

And he was going to see Natasha that afternoon. Stupid. All he had to do was call and say no. A mistake. A onetime fall. A onetime fall guy. No, all his fault. A fault so deep it was geological. Shit. Karen didn't deserve... He saw the line of traffic up ahead. He told himself not to be so hard on himself. He promised not to be. And Natasha's touch and smell. Her sounds. Silk honey and sandalwood musk

and how she moved. The things she said as she
moved, moved him.

He was moving slowly in a line of traffic over the
canal bridge. Oh, to be off the road. To be in an open
boat! He looked up the canal. It was jammed with a
long unmoving line of boats.

〰〰〰〰 **9**

The house was small and had too many windows,
was cluttered with small windows and had a wooden
sign saying JANSEN—HATMAKER in the Regency re-
vival letters of the 1920s.

He rang the bell. Piano music from the back. Schumann? He rang the bell again.

"I'm coming, I'm coming," came a tinkly old
woman's voice. The door opened. She was maybe
four foot eleven, in plaid shirt and chinos and round
and with a tanned face so lined and eyes so bright
brown and deep set that she looked like a chocolate
chip cookie.

"Why, yes, hello," she said loudly and giggled.

Schwartz couldn't help giggling back, looked at the
slip of paper and asked to see Fran Jansen, the hatmaker.

"Why, yes, come in. That's me."

They stepped into the showroom. Schwartz and the woman. He looked again. Or Schwartz and the man.

"Richard Cooke gave me your name. He said—"

"Oh, yes, Richard. Jan? Jan! Here's a friend of Richard Cooke come to visit. Jan?"

Perhaps the introduction would clear things up.

At the back end of the showroom was a flight of stairs much too large for the house down which lumbered a tall, burly old man in plaid shirt and chinos.

He stopped before Schwartz and looked down at him with the same cookie face but much larger—one of those giant chocolate chips, except that the end of his flat nose was a nearly spherical pale red bump, as if an unripe plum had accidentally fallen into the batch.

"Jan, this here is Richard Cooke's friend, who hasn't told me his name."

"Oh, Len Schwartz." He'd skip the police business. The police business was getting him nowhere. No—in trouble was where.

The two looked at him; he looked at them. Then he looked from the strange looking tall person to the strange looking short person and knew he couldn't tell if they were husband and wife, or wife and wife, or husband and husband or twins of one or more genders. So he looked at the elaborate, beautiful hats, very stylish, too, in 1927, '37, '47 and '57, where all styles seemed to end. And there were racks of identical large oval hatboxes printed with a horse before an English rose cottage where he wouldn't mind being right now.

"You were good friends of Victor Amboys?"

"Not talking about Victor, Len Schwartz," said the tall one, loudly, in the same old lady pitch as the other.

And he or she turned to a hatstand and flicked a long yellow feather.

"Stop shouting, Jan. That music's too loud. Why don't you turn it down?"

Not Schumann. "That's Schubert, isn't it?" asked Schwartz.

"What did you say?" shouted the big one, stepping very close to him.

"I said Schubert."

"Holy smokes you're right! Most people would've guessed Schumann. They'd've been wrong. How'd you know? You a pianist?"

"No, but I like music. It's that maybe because he wasn't a great pianist, the music isn't so flashy, like he had to make sure the melody and harmony were so good. I mean, I don't know."

"Fran? You hear this man? Isn't this man something?"

"Well, sure, cookie. Richard wouldn't send over no dope."

Cookie? Did he hear one call the other *cookie*?

The big one said, "No dope? I'll say, cookie. Come on up, Len, then."

"To our den," the short one chimed, rhymed in.

Schwartz followed. Cookie and cookie. Had he wandered into the gingerbread house? Upstairs it was no gingerbread house; it was a grand salon in which any number of Jamesian exchanges might have been pleased to occur. The little house downstairs was a shop added to this. . . . Of course, an old converted potato barn.

And this, its top half, was a room a hundred by fifty with oriental carpets and groups of sofas, tables and chairs, tall standing lamps and shawls and chandeliers.

A grand piano, sculpture, books, photos in old frames . . .

"Well," Fran said, "sit down anywheres looks comfy and, heavens, Janny, turn down that music, Schubert or—"

"Schubert or *Showboat*, Franny. Ha hee!" And big Jan stamped over to the phonograph, turned it off and came to sit at the other end of the sofa from Schwartz and said, "Enough of this joking around. Sure. I'll tell you. Man knows Schubert from Schumann can damn well know whatever he wants about Vic Amboys."

"Well, shoot," said Fran, loudly, smiling on a chair across from Schwartz.

Since this was clearly the opening night of a Feydeau farce or something by Oscar Wilde, except the accents were all wrong, he might as well shoot. "Did Victor Amboys ever tell you about a lost Shinnecock deed he'd discovered?"

"Oh, sure," said Fran.

"Not lost, neither. Was hidden from them—stole!" said Jan, eyes widening and mouth opening toothless, a puckered gingerbread.

"Did he say what land?" Schwartz couldn't believe his luck. He leaned back; they were so informal. Should he put his feet up on the table?

"Why, would you believe, the Russia community back there Sag Harbor way," Jan said.

Fran said, "Isn't Sag Harbor, more Noyack."

"Not Noyack neither, more where that Bridgehampton car racing used to go on," said Jan.

Schwartz was charmed. He relaxed.

"Hey," said Jan, "you're not taking to put your feet up on that, are you?"

"Holy smokes, don't. That's Hepplewhite," Fran said, smiling.

"Well, almost, Fran. Actually a turn-of-the-century copy. Call it Stanford Hepple White. Pretty good, huh?"

"Pretty good, all right, Jan," said Fran. "It's also pretty old."

"So's the table, Fran. But I was saying how Vic said he'd come across this deed and was going to try getting that land back to the Shinnecock Indians. And I think he could of, 'cause his idea was to go right to the old Kalubins and Glebors over at the Russia art place and, darn, they would've probably have given it back, long as they could stay there the rest of their lives, I figure. Vic did too. Hey, Len, you think we're old coots you should go over there see them."

"Nice folks, though," Fran put in.

"Didn't say different, cookie," said Jan.

Fran asked, "Then Vic got sad, didn't he?"

"Sad and scared, Len. Vic said he was being kept away from seeing the old folks. Said it looked like he'd have to take it to law or something. Then—"

"Then he got killed on the beach," Fran said in the same loud, bright voice, but large tears dropped from the chocolate eyes.

"We miss him, Len," Jan continued in the identical high bluster, with the identical tears.

Schwartz asked, "Did he ever say where the deed was?"

"Sure," Fran said. "Said he was always keeping it right on him case anyone took to break into his cottage to steal it. Let's see; maybe there was something else, but I can't remember."

"How about an apple?" asked Jan.

"Or some whiskey. You like whiskey? We got gin

too. Sometimes we like whiskey, other times we like gin. Don't know why."

"Isn't the weather," said Jan.

"Heck, no; gin's good in winter," said Fran.

"When we're in a gin mood, Franny."

"No, thanks. I have to be going. Here's my number. If you think of anything else. You've been very helpful. I'd better explain why—"

"Don't bother," said Fran.

"No need," said Jan. "You're okay, Len. We know. You come up anytime and we'll get drunk and hear some Schubert. And we'll tell you if anything else comes to us about Vic."

Schwartz stood to leave the dream room.

"Say," said Fran, "you want to see the family?"

"Oh, now, Fran's always showing off the kids and grandkids."

Schwartz held his breath so the bubble charm wouldn't break. He looked at the photos Fran held out. Children, grandchildren—definitely theirs. Chocolate chips off the old block.

They went down the grand stairs and through the Beatrix Potter shop and stood at the door.

"Bye, now, Len," said Fran, arm around the big shambling Jan. "Hope you didn't think we were carrying on too bad. We grump some, but this here's the best wife any man ever had," he said, leaning his little cookie head against his wife's long side.

10

Under a weeping willow by the pond, Schwartz sat near the tombstone. The scene wanted only an urn and some clothing other than his cutoffs and old sneakers to be an eighteenth-century memorial print. It wasn't; it was ten minutes down the broad East Hampton street from meeting Natasha, and all he could think of were various conversations over the years with Karen concerning to what extent he regarded her as not only his wife but his mother. Early on he'd said not at all, not a jot nor an iota. Later, he'd admitted to some.

She'd said, "Stay out of trouble," and what had her bad boy done? Without her only five days and by day three he'd managed to put a man into allergic shock, and the man had been his guest and perhaps important to Karen's career. And this he'd done by rubbing the man with poison ivy, as he'd done when he was nine years old to his cousin Harvey Silverman. Wonderful.

And why? Wasn't it because in this little nursery drama Soloff took the role of daddy, making him, nice little Oedipus, so jealous? (This is my son the King. Oi, he's terrific with riddles. Come, come here, Oedipusel. Don't be so bashful all of a sudden. You know Mrs. Sphinx from the sixth floor. Ask, Mildred, ask, you'll see. Oedipuselah, don't be such a baby. What do you think, she'll bite you? Throw you out the window?)

And by day four of Karen's absence, he'd been unfaithful. He'd DONE IT with another. Ah, *"done it,"* the words from his childhood, so inarticulate and potent. He had taken another into Karen's marriage bed. But if Karen was his mother . . .

Schwartz jumped to his feet. He was making it a word game again, a joke book. What he had to do was to get out of this elegant village and its goofy Englishness.

He was driving farther into town. He could turn off anywhere. He passed the grand elm trees being treated against blight, plastic tubes tapped in and out of their thick trunks like IV's into old folks—conditions terminal but still plugged in to expensive, intensive care.

"I do! I care intensively!" he yelled in the car and turned it around and drove back home feeling better.

And worse. Was he a man or a mouse? A man, of course. But what would the mice say?

Are you a mouse or a man?

A mouse!

Well, damn it, act like one, then!

He rang Brooklyn on the off chance. Nothing. He rang MOMA and was shunted from extension to extension until someone said yes, she had seen Ms. Walker around earlier and would try to find her and did, tried but couldn't find her—perhaps she was still at lunch or had left.

Schwartz rang Natasha. Her mother answered.

"Is this Len?"

"Yes, I . . ."

"This is Helen Kalubin, you remember. We met. Natasha's in East Hampton. She said she was meeting you there, I thought half an hour ago."

"Me? Oh, yes, there was an idea to meet to discuss certain . . . Well, matters pertaining to this . . ."

"Len?"

"Yes?"

"You don't have to pretend. We're very close, Natasha and I. We discuss everything."

"I don't quite understand. Everything? Uh, please tell Natasha I'm unable to make it. Sorry. I can't. Thank you."

"But . . ."

"Goodbye now." He stood with his hand on the phone thinking that no one could accuse him of not acting like a mouse in defense of his manhood.

He nibbled at a cheese sandwich. He stripped and jumped into the pool. No relief; it felt warm and oily, like swimming in chicken soup. He looked at the volumes of Tolstoy and decided he didn't like Tolstoy. A terrible admission, but there it was. He'd read what he damn well pleased—a book as frivolous as those striped shirts at Saks. There, just the thing—Dostoyevsky's *From the House of the Dead*. Yes, that would be good for a few chuckles by poolside.

He napped with the book opened on his face and woke in its smothering shadow. The sun had sunk below the trees. He put on shorts and sneakers and went out running.

He came back and stood dripping with sweat at the phone. He imagined it ringing on their hall table in Park Slope. Ring, ring, ring, under Baskin's noble Indian. But he knew it was beneath its dignity to answer.

After he showered he made more calls to the city. Ed and Bob hadn't heard from Karen, nor had Annie, nor had Jack. Millie had. Millie hawed, hemmed and said she'd had lunch with Karen at the museum and it wasn't that Karen had said anything, and it wasn't probably any of her business, but Karen had seemed very angry and hurt and said she was going to take a few days off to think, but nothing more specific than that. And if she could be of any help . . .

He thanked Millie.

What did it mean? What did it mean?

Ten minutes later Natasha telephoned and told him what. "Natasha, what do you mean, 'Karen knows'? Is there closed-circuit TV between this bedroom and Park Slope?"

Natasha said, "Darling. I understand your surprise, but it's really all for the best. I am sorry it all happened before I could tell you, but you didn't show up at Dolce Vita. And then just as I got home Karen called to speak to Alexei about some documents concerning Grandpa's paintings, so I thought it was a good opportunity to get on the phone and tell her. I couldn't stand deceiving her."

Schwartz heard himself whispering, "Ahhh."

"What, darling? So I said we were having an affair. More lust than love and I said I knew how much you really loved her and told her how I liked her so much and if we tried we could understand each other. All of us."

"You *said* that?"

"Yes, darling. Certainly. I don't want to break up your marriage."

"No need. I'm doing that very well on my own. Look, Natasha—you're very sweet and good and slightly off your Slavic skull and . . . If Karen calls you, don't say . . . Don't . . . She may not quite see this as the jolly romp you do. Jesus! What did she say? I didn't even think to . . . What did she say?"

"She was nice, darling. Quiet. She said yes, yes, I see. Like that."

"Ahhh. Natasha, give me twenty minutes or half an hour at most to sort out the rest of my life on this planet and I'll get back to you."

"All right, darling. It will be all right. Listen to me. I know."

He put the phone down. She knows. Oh, then that's fine. She knows! What? Why? Why her? Why after twenty faithful years do I choose to sleep with someone who mainlines sodium pentothal?

One very clear idea came to him. He'd call Tom Gallagher, ask him to initiate formal investigation proceedings based on what he'd found, and he'd step out of this business so he could have all his energy to try saving his marriage. Right.

But the phone rang.

"Leonard Schwartz?"

"Yes?"

"Unicorn Baldock, here. My dear fellow, this is jolly awkward but what's a host to do, eh? Your charming wife has asked me to call so that you won't be worried or start a police search. She's fine and here with us at the Manor House."

"Oh?"

"Arrived a short while ago. We're delighted to have her. You know, she's researching those cute paintings Mother bought from Kalubin and the Glebors in the twenties and thirties."

"Yes. May I speak to her."

"Ah. Now, ah. Dear fellow, that's the point. She's a bit, you know. A bit. And so she asked me to talk to you. Said she'd be staying here for at least a few days. An honor for me, of course. Her book is simply *the* best—"

"Who else is staying?"

"Hmm? Oh, absolutely no one. Oh, Valodya, of course. But he's really like family, so I don't . . . Oh, well, just between you and me and you mustn't breathe a word—we are expecting . . . But you mustn't tell because Madame *déteste profondément* publicity— Miss—"

"Mr. Baldock, I don't care. I expected Karen back on Saturday, the day after tomorrow. Please tell her I'll call her then. And if I don't get to speak with her, I think I'll come visiting."

"My dear man, how passionate! I love it. You sound just like . . ."

Schwartz didn't slam the phone; he put it down gently, and Unicorn Baldock's voice slurred away.

Shits, those shits. And I'm the worst of the lot. His clear idea about calling Gallagher and saving his marriage began to cloud. And the doorbell was ringing. Oh, yes, it would have to be. It couldn't be worse. Oh, yes. He went to let Natasha in.

"Ginger?"

"Hello, Len. Have a few minutes? I think we should talk," Whelehan said.

"Yes, well . . . Yes. For a few minutes, anyhow. I'm . . ." Schwartz said, letting it hang as he ushered Whelehan in and listened for Natasha's car.

Whelehan made himself very comfortable in one of the big white armchairs, his briefcase beside him. Yes, very comfortable and casual in his brown-and-white-striped seersucker suit and summery shirt, doubtless from Saks. Schwartz hovered nervously.

"Very, very nice place Mr. Childs has. Serious security."

Jesus, Natasha could show up any minute."Yes. Well, if you could come to the point. As I said, I—"

"A place like this is part of the point. I intend to have a place like this."

Why did all the loons zoom in on him? "That's nice, Ginger. But I don't see—"

"You think I shouldn't? Because I'm a cop? Just a sergeant? Maybe because I didn't go to Hahvahd?"

"No, I don't think—"

"It's okay, is it, for someone who went to a small Catholic college?"

"Ginger, um, I graduated in the sixties when people who went to Harvard were regularly arrested by people who went to small Catholic colleges. And, you know, I seem to remember that Bob Childs didn't even finish college. So it looks good for you, that way, I mean."

"And these pictures, paintings—I know most of them. That's a Rosenquist and that's a Stella. Surprised?"

Oh, yes, the Plimpton syndrome. "Delighted. You've come here to talk art. Great. I'm okay, but Karen's really so much better. But you know that."

"Let me put it this way: Do you have a video machine here?"

What was this? Was the man moonlighting in broad daylight, selling videos door-to-door? "Yes. I think. We don't . . . Over there, under the TV."

"I'd like to show you . . ." said Ginger, opening his briefcase and taking out a videocassette. "Like to take this opportunity to show you . . ." he said, fiddling with the machine.

What would this be, an arty video, a grainy documentary of Ginger controlling the crowds chez Plimpton on the Fourth of July? Did he want help finding a commercial backer, maybe Bob? Even as he asked the questions, he began to know.

"Here it comes, Len."

Oh, yes, it would be . . . White screen, nothing and then. Yes. The house, the pool, Karen naked, himself naked, Karen getting up, sitting on his lap.

"Len, I don't think this investigation of yours can do either of us any good."

Outrageous. How long had he been videotaping? "Ginger, this is not—"

"Listen! I've done nothing wrong. There's nothing in this business but the usual. I mean, everyone's trying to make it their own way. Like you. Like my Uncle Tom. Sure, I help people out. Sure, they give me land-investment tips. I know you've found that out. So what? It's all legal. I don't run with gangsters or drug dealers, Len."

The screen was blank again. Good. It was like pornography, watching his wife and himself like that. "What has Gallagher been—"

"My uncle has nothing to do with this. I've found out certain things on my own. Oh, wait. Here comes scene two. Same location, same leading man, only there's a new bi . . . leading lady."

It was Natasha at the poolside. She walked toward him; he . . . Had he grabbed her so fast? But there they were kissing. Ginger would have been sharp enough to have made copies. No use destroying this one. Well, what else? Oh, lovely. Sweet, the two of them naked at the bedroom window like that. Only a few seconds but focused and unmistakable. Then the curtains. Curtains.

Well, at least now he needn't worry about Natasha showing up.

"So I'd really be grateful if you stopped all this. It doesn't even concern you. You know it's Uncle Tom doing some Albany scumbag a favor," Ginger said, not even looking Schwartz's way, crouched to press the rewind button. "What do you say, Len?"

He could kill him, of course, but he'd never afford the dry cleaning of Bob's white carpets. "Well, Ginger, I think you shot it with a bit too much blue filter, though that shot of me at the window is kind of cute. Rather Attic vase-like, what with my dark skin and what would have been in days of yore called my upright manhood, though hood might not be it as I'm circumcised. Ginger —this is Harvard for 'No, indeed.' I'm calling your bluff."

Ginger put the cassette back into the briefcase. It was a good briefcase; the latches made sharp neat clicks as he shut them. "Have it your way, but it won't be worth it."

"Well, what's a Greek urn, anyway? Right, Ginger? And there's the door, Ginger."

"All right. So long. I just thought as we're fellow police I'd do the right thing."

"And you have, Ginger, as far as I'm concerned. Just the right thing," Schwartz said, aware he hadn't the slightest idea of what he meant.

He closed the door very quietly and stood there until the car drove off. The cloudy idea about calling Gallagher and saving his marriage was driven off with it.

BOOK III

1

Karen had said she'd be away for a week. This was the sixth day and still no call. If he thought about things like that, he could make coffee without spilling it. Yes, this way his guilt could slip quietly into the shadow of his great male anger at Karen's island incommunicado. He added a second mug to the tray.

Yes, Detective, except for the clue of the second mug, your alibi for anger would be believable—cheap, but believable. There were, however, two cream-white mugs patterned with flamingos. He also was a big nosed lovebird. Yeah, but he had better legs. The coffee was spilling.

Seeing Natasha through the open door shocked him. She sat up in bed running her hands through her hair—sleepy, smiling and beautiful. And he decided he was shocked because she wasn't Karen. He was, yes, offending himself. Why did he need to do this: displacement? Adultery as the lesser guilt?

"That smells nice," Natasha said as he set the tray on the bed between them.

As Tristan set the sword between him and fair Iseult, so Schwartz did set two cups of Zabar's pure Colombian. And the sword hadn't worked, either.

She said, "I like your mugs." As good a straight line

111

as could be expected, yet he didn't say "I like yours too" or any of its infinite yet stale variety because this was Natasha where Karen should be. Was it Karen he disliked this much or himself? If himself, why was his punishment to give himself such pleasure?

"Leonard, you look sad and guilty and you shouldn't. You'll see, we'll work this out. Karen will work this out on the island. She'll return. . . . But you'd rather not have me talk about her."

"Yes, no. Please." He held the mug to his face. The birds were stuck. He turned it. The birds were going round in circles. He'd walked in circles outside the high white fence until he located the tree from which Cecil B. DeWhelehan had shot his mini-blockbuster, his homebuster, "Lenny and the Sixth Commandment."

"How is it you can be so warm to me in bed—I also mean the things you said to me last night—and now you're so cold?"

"I've come down with a severe case of ambivalence."

"Darling, the important thing is not to mope. Why don't we go to the beach?"

Natasha leaned across the tray and put her hands on his shoulders. "Come on." She smiled, she tilted her head, she made a funny face. "You look so young when you smile," she said. "We'll go to Dolce Vita and get some picnic and go out to the beach." She massaged his shoulders. "All right?"

It wasn't. There was Whelehan out there peddling blue Schwartz films door-to-door. Or not—saving them for some large-screen occasion. And there was nothing he could do. It was not all right. Still, it might be that Natasha was acting on Soloff's behalf, could link the mad Russian with Troost or Whelehan. Yes, the investigation. Yes, his research. such selflessness! Besides, since Karen already knew ... He said, "All right."

They parked in the lot near the A&P and walked across Long Lane. Why shop at a normal supermarket when for six times the price you could convince yourself you were in the Hamptons because the Hamptons was where you complained about how expensive the food was? He explained this to Natasha as they approached the Ritz-rustic facade of Dolce Vita. She said yes, but they were going there.

And then, quickly: "Or if you don't want." She stopped. "Let's go back to—"

"No, Dolce Vita will be fine."

"Now, Leonard, behave!"

"Absolutely. Mirror of courtliness," he said, coming up to the tall bearded man who rocked on his toes and smiled at them sweetly in the Dolce Vita doorway.

"Natasha, my dear. Leonard. Good morning."

"Good morning, Valodya," she said, giving her cheek as he bent to kiss her.

Schwartz nodded. He was being nice. He'd say something nice. "You look better."

"Thank you, my friend. I owe this to you. My getting better, I mean. Your presence of mind to take me for emergency treatment."

"Not at all. My pleasure. And thank you, Vladimir, for whatever I owe you. I mean my current position, this refuge you've helped provide for my wife."

"Ah, yes. Well, such is life. Now one, now another. Now it's you who has—how do you say—has egg on his face?"

"Come, darling," Natasha said, her hand on Schwartz's arm. "Good-bye, Valodya."

Schwartz wondered who Soloff was waiting for. For Karen? If he saw Karen what would he do? Would he still be nice? And had that "darling" from Natasha been her artless heart or a sophisticated signal to Soloff? And all this assonance and alliteration was a sure sign of his nerves.

The store was crowded with weekend providers who thrilled to everything so understated and overpriced.

"You get what you want for us; I'll walk around. But I'm paying," said Schwartz.

"Don't be silly."

"Yes, I insist," he said, and walked off. He was paying.

He stopped before a table of vegetables. He knew they were for salads, but that was it. There were possible lettuces with names that in his glance read like "Grounique" and, but this couldn't be right, "Albigensian Stoy (California)" and prices like nobody's business. Well, nobody but Dolce Vita's.

He returned to Natasha, who was attending a short unpleasant lecture given by an eighteen-year-old professor of cheese vending.

"We shouldn't take the *torte dolcelatte* to the beach. Not so much the gorgonzola but the cream layers would become runny, and we think the genius of the cheese is its consistency, as well as taste."

The genius of the cheese? The genius? Schwartz looked. It appeared smart, but not *that* smart. He whispered to Natasha, "At his age I'd barely ventured from Velveeta to a tentative Monterey Jack." And he added to young snotty, "The first time I heard of a store called Dolce Vita I thought it sold sweet herring."

"Yes? Now, what would you like, madam?"

"Natasha, get something simple and seaworthy like a Port Salute."

"Salut," said Toffeenose.

"Salot," said Schwartz, walking away.

Stainless steel, slick cookbooks, racks of bland British biscuits and there was the back of Soloff's head through the window and his hand up by his beard waving to someone, but, no, waving someone away, across the street.

But by the time Schwartz moved up to the window, whoever had disappeared. Karen?

He was still trying to be nice, but this place would seem gross to Lucullus: pink-white elephant garlic looking like the stranger's neck goiter you stare at even as you tell yourself you mustn't; boysenberry vinegars to go with oil of macadamia to go with, naturally, those pretty wicker trays of wild mushrooms.

"I would think you'd had enough of those, my friend."

Soloff stood beside him with a smile of such angelic openness that it was difficult for Schwartz not to kick the big creep.

"Vladimir, in my work I've learned to keep sticking my nose back in, even when the business really stinks."

"Ah, yes. And it's true, isn't it, friend, that sometimes such smells stick? But you'll excuse me. I must pick up some caviar—for a small dinner party tonight at the Manor."

What did he mean, "such smells stick"? Was that a random insult or . . . The bribe inquiry? Who told him? Did Whelehan really know or was it Karen? What about that cozy dinner with Karen? Karen and caviar. And what did he mean, calling him "friend"?

Schwartz pushed back into the store past men with big bellies and small packages. In cases behind them, salamis were dark red and shiny, their bits of fat flecked white like blisters. Soloff was at the end of a counter where two ordinarily mandarin salespersons in smart chocolate colored smocks now nodded and scraped and nearly snorted with the pleasure of serving the Great Man.

Schwartz approached muttering, "Kow-tow, brown sow." The two elegant pigs, not so much sows as crashing bores, bent under the counter and did a strange backward scurry through a door. It was becoming very hard to be nice.

"Soloff, a favor: please don't call me 'friend,' especially in public. My reputation, you understand."

"Of course. But I thought your reputation was that of a friend to drug dealers."

Schwartz thought he saw the end of Soloff's flat nose twitch. Something strange was happening. The nose was laughing at him. Karen? God, had Karen told Soloff about . . . Had she told him in bed? In bed with Soloff, afterward, had she? Only the nose knew. The nose in this store made it impossible to be nice.

"Well, Inspector?" asked the nose.

Now Schwartz understood. No more Mr. Niceboy Tolstoy. He was the Inspector General and he didn't like Tolstoy. It was Gogol or nothing. He said, "I challenge your nose to a duel."

Soloff's nose made the mistake of lifting its eyebrow. Schwartz picked a tiny chocolate truffle from a bowl. It was priced one dollar and seventy-five cents and was dusted with confectioners' sugar. Schwartz blew the sugar onto the nose's raspberry-pink shirt so that it made a small white botch over its heart.

"Am I to take this white powder as a symbol of your —reputation, Inspector?"

The nose snapped its fingers and hissed. Another chocolate-covered sales snot appeared. A very fat man had begun to spectate. He wore a green and red Benetton sweatshirt with the word SAVE on it in large black letters. The word rose and fell on the man's big breasts.

When the Liederkranz arrived, and Schwartz knew that Liederkranz was the perfect choice, the nose, or more exactly, the nose's nose, sniffed at it delicately, nodded—had two hundred and fifty grams weighed, wrapped and priced—took it from the attendant, pulled off the price tag, opened the bag, unrolled the wrapping paper and then the clear wrap, put its index finger into the cheese, came up with a three-quarter-inch-long and quarter-inch-wide glistening yellow blob, sniffed it once more and nodding and smiling politely drew the cheese slowly across Schwartz's cheek, beginning just behind his ear and ending with a small, spinning flourish under his right nostril.

Schwartz smiled and bowed. "Touché."

"Merely a return."

"But a ripe one," said Schwartz, seeing that another man had joined the fat one, a man with a blond mustache and a bagful of baguettes. And at the other end of the counter there was Natasha, shaking her head no, miming out the words *YOU PROMISED*, her mouth open, lips pouting beautifully after the *PR* . . . and prettily pursed at the *M*. . . .

Three women stopped. Schwartz said good morning

They said nothing; they had their cheek. Schwartz had his; they stared at it.

Now the two staff reappeared from the back carrying a large Styrofoam box between them which they set on the floor before the counter. As they took off its cover a haze of dry ice lifted in a small cloud. They removed another large Styrofoam box and set it on the counter top and from it took a jar, of heavy earthenware, approximately eighteen inches high and nine inches across.

The nose was attempting to communicate something to the attendants, but it either spoke too sotto voce or too much through its nose so that they continued unwrapping the tape, lifting off the plastic and finally the jar's heavy lid.

There was a small gasp from the crowd, like the sound of an ancient casino when, despite its great wealth or because of it, the tiaraed and tuxedoed crowd around the roulette table sees a giant jackpot pushed some player's way. Just so, the gasp from the deli shoppers at the epic tub of fresh black beluga before them.

The nose was shaking its head no. And yet, of course, it knew. Perhaps it always knew.

"May I?" Schwartz asked pleasantly of the staff, who smiled and stepped back for his better perusal.

"Thank you," he said, and stuck in both hands and came up with gobs and pushed them into the nose's nose and eyes and mouth then jumped behind the nose and got it into a half nelson (seeing Natasha and a redheaded man rushing his way) and bending the arm he bent the nose's head down and down through the yelling and "Oh no"s into the tub and rubbed it and dubbed it down there.

And as a hand touched him he turned and said, "Whelehan, nice to see you without the video sales kit. I thought you were in hiding across the street."

"Six thousand dollars! That's six thousand dollars of caviar you've ruined!" screamed one of the smooth staff, his voice ruffled and rougher. The other said, "I'm calling the police."

That ended the spell. Soloff was only Soloff again. But he had a beard dyed black, glistening dripping caviar, really magnificent, like an allegorical figure—Triton himself but for the spitting, hawking and the drooling of black slime.

"We are the police. That's the rub. Isn't that right, Whelehan? Charge this to the Southampton police. The sergeant here will take down the particulars," said Schwartz to everyone—the laughers, the gaspers, Natasha come with paper towels to dab at Soloff, the grumblers and, most, to the scared-stiff majority.

Schwartz, on his way out to nowhere, said, "Whelehan, your buddy's got egg on his face."

————— 2

He pushed at the pile of cracked records on the floor with a fluted table leg. Stanford Hepple White. They called each other "cookie." Not a painting, not a photo left intact. He watched Gallagher move around the

smashed grand piano—the toothless keyboard, a wild
cowlick of snapped wires out its top.

"Well?"

"I'm glad you called me first, Lenny, but we're
gonna have to let those local people in here in a few
minutes."

"For what? For prints?"

"Yeah, or whatever."

"Want to bet?"

"No."

"No," said Schwartz, who kept pushing the rubble on
the floor with the table leg. "Nothing missing here, no
prints, a thoroughly professional job."

"Any ideas?" asked Gallagher, looking into the stuff-
ing of a slashed sofa for nothing particular.

"Is this the procedure, Tom? I'm to tell you what
you know? Okay. Fran Jansen calls last night to tell
me they've remembered something more about
Amboys, and why don't I come over for lunch today
to discuss it. Then, sometime during the night . . . And
when I get here—this, and those two nice people
dumb with shock. That's the very fine touch, not a
hair out of place on either of them. And the house,
well . . . I know it's not so close to others, but no one
in the neighborhood heard anything, and it's like a
bomb's gone off in here. Tremendously professional
work, wouldn't you say?"

"Yeah, yeah. All right, so you suspect Ginger. How
do you think—"

"Enough, Tom. I don't have the patience." Schwartz
set the table leg onto the wreckage of the table.
"Ginger's into a phone tap."

"He has a phone tap on you?" Gallagher asked, continuing to look away from Schwartz.

"I said he was *into* a phone tap. *You* have a phone tap on me. He's into that. Tom?"

Gallagher lifted his head and stepped toward Schwartz. His big feet crunched broken china; his mouth opened as if to yell. A sigh came out. "Yeah, I do. To protect us, Lenny. Honest. Tabs to keep it all . . . Believe me. Shit, I'm carrying the can on this."

Schwartz thought of Whelehan's videos in the can, but he didn't want to toss that one out to Gallagher. He'd stick with the phone and Whelehan always a step or three ahead. "Maybe something will be missing, some cover to make it look like burglary," he said, seeing how the glass in a broken photo frame pushed a jagged line through Jansen grandchildren. "Whelehan could have gotten to your tap. You trust your tap?"

"You're asking if I trust Dick Brennan."

Schwartz looked across to a window. No, they wouldn't break the windows. "Ah, the clean provincial ear of Albany. Some heavyweight favor at state level."

"I didn't say that, and you're better off not knowing."

Schwartz felt light-headed, but maybe that was still his liver or his kidneys. "Sure, Tom. Your reasons for keeping me in the dark are always so politically impeccable. Right, let's not waste time arguing style. Somehow Whelehan's tapped in and I'm a miracle of patience in not shooting him dead at noon on Job's Lane. And do we go for him or do we wait for him to frame another retarded non-white adolescent for this?"

"Fuck you, Lenny. I hate this, too, and I am not protecting Ginger or anyone except maybe you and me. We don't have shit on Ginger. This is his turf, and if he was careless with the Johnson kid he sure as hell is gonna be careful now. We need some hard evidence. Sure, we could go to an investigation now, and it would drag on and they'd close ranks here and the upshot would be maybe there'd be some cautions or probations and that would fucking well be that, just like you've been saying. Look, let's get over to the hospital and see how your friends are coming along. Maybe they'll talk despite—this. What's that?"

"Some piano music. A broken record. Nothing."

At the bottom of the stairs they thanked the waiting Southampton police for giving them the five minutes. Chief Beck said sure, and he understood and he was going to handle this personally. And Schwartz and Gallagher exchanged a glance concerning the eloquent absence of Detective Whelehan.

At the hospital they were told to wait. Then they were told that both Jansens had been mildly sedated and were asleep. Then Schwartz demanded to see them so that he saw that Jan was asleep and then he crossed the corridor and saw that Fran was asleep. He thought both were trembling slightly, a flutter he saw under their eyelids. Out in the corridor it came to him that that's how the cookies crumbled, and the funniness of this idea made him walk away from Gallagher and go around the corner and put his cheek to the cool white wall.

Gallagher's blue Lincoln drove off without Schwartz having answered "Anything else you want to tell me?" and without Schwartz having asked about the tapes that Brennan inadvertently made available to Tom: little talks with Natasha and with Natasha's mother, all the searching for Karen. He didn't care. He wanted Karen back. He'd played out his guilty little Liebestod with

Natasha. He needed Karen. And today was the day he'd bragged about going out to Baldock Island to get her. What a he-man!

He started the Volvo. He man and she Jane. The motor gave a deep roar. He schmuck and it was all his fault. Except that now, besides a murder, theft, conspiracy and fraud, there was also ... What whould you call it, what Whelehan had done to the Jansens? Some sort of rape.

All he wanted was his much wronged wife to talk with and a glass of milk. And if the milk stood for mother comfort, well, let it.

God, the house was so slick and cold and *Better Homes & Gardens* empty. At least he had his music. He put on a sad, warm Shostakovich quartet and went to the kitchen.

As he closed it the milk carton caught his eye. This missing kid was Robert Mackery. Date missing, 9/4/82; from Framingham, MA; DOB, 6/11/75; White Male; Eyes, Brown; Height, 4'; Weight, 44; Hair, Brown. The large-eyed child looked blurred and wistful in the blown-up family photo.

Schwartz thought he knew this kid's chances. He'd seen one or two of them discovered, uncovered. He'd seen how they'd been used—stripped, peeled, split, discarded.

You couldn't, Jesus, you couldn't even drink a glass of milk anymore. The victims looked out at you from everywhere. They...

When Karen came in he was sitting weeping on the kitchen floor with the full glass of milk clasped in both hands.

3

Karen drank a glass of water by the sink. She passed the back of her hand across her lips. "I thought," she said, "to ask you if you had a nice week. I was going to begin with that. But I see it ... it hasn't been ..." She took a long breath, damned if she'd cry.

He stopped. "Whatever you have to ask, the answer is yes. Yes, I slept with Natasha. Yes, it was out of boredom or jealousy or self-loathing or out of whatever you say it was, yes. I'm sorry. I'm so sorry. I didn't imagine it would be so physical, a lump of lead, here," he said quietly, pressing the bottom of his chest.

"What do you mean, whatever I say?" She spoke even more quietly than he had. "You're not going to preempt me like that, like whatever I feel or say you've already felt or said for me. Prepaid guilt and contrition and then you can just nod your sad little lamb's head and feel so satisfied hearing me echo your own wise thoughts."

Her voice came louder. "No, Len, not this time. It's happened too much these last few years. You act foully and you're called on it and you confess your little-lamb soul out—and that's supposed to be it. All gone. All the nastiness and dirt washed clean away. And do you know it's me too?"

"What?"

"Me, me! I go down the drain with it. Somehow I'm left outside your sulks and angers—and now your betrayal and I'm . . ." Her voice broke. She slapped her hand on the steel drainboard. "I will not be preempted! My misery is real. The way you've made me feel like dirt is real. I won't keep silent. You are not going to speak for me; you're not going to choke me with your tears."

"I'm sorry. Karen, I'm sorry. This case . . . Two sweet old people have—"

"No! No! No! It may be awful but it will have to wait; I'll have to be sorry about it later. Do you understand? Don't do this. Don't throw your murders at me. Don't hide behind . . . For God's sake, stop hiding behind corpses! I'm here. I'm alive! Do you understand?"

Her breath came hard, as if she were running uphill. "Alive!" she yelled. "I'm here, alive. Tend to the living. The dead are dead, you bastard! You ghoulish petty bastard!"

Crouched, he saw the glass flash at the end of her arm and ducked to the side. It smashed against the refrigerator. He stood and went to calm her.

"Don't touch me. You touch me, you dare and—"

"Calm down."

"No. No! I've calmed down too much for you. You think your touch is some magic solace? It's not."

"How about Soloff's?"

"What? How dare . . . Oh, go to hell. When your wonderfully sincere girlfriend told me, I didn't believe it—although deep down I suppose I knew it was true, because sooner or later... But then her mother, her *mother* tells me how it's true and how we all have to love each other and suffer! Oh, Jesus, Mary and Joseph, it would be funny if it didn't hurt so much. And yes. Yes, I needed solace. And I got it—the solace of work, which is what I was doing on Baldock Island. Oh, and the solace of extra cocktails and wine and being pampered. But that's all. That's all, so far. But who knows? Vladimir's attractive and maybe you'll convince me of the great solace of fucking around. Or is that just okay for a real guy, like you?"

"No, it's no solace."

"Really? Where? Where'd you get this no solace? In our bed?"

"Karen, don't—"

"Too sordid? Don't 'don't' me! Where? Did you fuck her here in the kitchen? The laundry? Did you play laundry with her? Did you tell her you loved her? Did she make your heart sing, you shit? Did she make it sing sad Russian songs like . . ."

Karen ran from the kitchen. The music stopped. He heard the clack of her nails against the plastic and the small whirring sounds which were the tape pulled and pulled from the cassette, and then he heard it crash.

He went in. "Shostakovich is innocent. It wasn't even Johnny Griffin. It was me, Karen. Please, let's talk." He walked toward her with open arms.

She turned and pulled cassettes from the shelf and threw them into his chest and face.

"All right. Stop. I won't—"

"Won't what—attack me? Use karate? Shoot me?"

"Won't do anything you don't . . . Look, I'll sit here. Please, sit and talk. Please."

Karen walked around the room and stopped by a

Rothko, black and purple like a bruise. "Yes. Talk. But no tricks, no schticks, no infant curly lamb charms."

"Yes. I'll try. Please."

She sat on the sofa opposite his chair. "Limits. There are limits! It's been hard for both of us since you took that cocaine bribe, but when I couldn't talk you out of it, I vowed to not let it ruin our lives. I think I'm a born optimist, but I'm telling you there are limits. I've tried to cheer you, to say let's get on with our lives, through the investigation, through all that time you were 'locked out,' as you put it. And it was miserable and hard very often, but I understood that and I could cope. So when you got that break last spring, a real case, an important one and then your success with it, and you got back into the life you wanted, I thought at last we could begin to . . . I was happy thinking you were and that we'd be more stable and . . . Why hasn't it worked for you?"

The question had come quietly. It seemed to slip under the net harboring his defenses. "It hasn't worked. That's right. It hasn't. Lots of reasons or a couple. You know how I liked being the department liberal, the bleeding heart, the softie intellectual? Well, since they brought me back into the action, last spring and now this case, it's . . . Don't you see? They use me like a land mine. Gallagher . . ."

"He forces you?"

"No. He doesn't have to; that's just it. They put me onto these impossible cases because they know my guilt makes me crazy enough to somehow—I don't know—at least neutralize otherwise untouchable criminals. I hate it. I hate that it's me. Me. My guilt produces this violence. It's horrible. And I was the official NYPD pacifist. Listen, it's like I'm not really

a detective anymore. They get a case of such clogged
filth that it won't budge and they call in Schwartz,
Mr. Roto-Rooter."

"And you think the guilt does this?"

"Yes, as if I was trying to hurt...No, to purge
myself. I mean, I want to punish myself, to hurt myself. Instead I project the violence out and by doing
so I also punish myself by offending my values.
And that clever bastard Gallagher knows. He uses it,
plays—"

"No. Don't! I am not getting drawn into another sterile discussion about whether he uses you or you use
him. This is about you and me—about how you've
used me. I want to know why. Why? Why did you do
this?" Karen's hand went into a fist that came down
hard on the glass coffee table.

She'd never been like this. But, then, he'd never...
He said, "Beside the guilt? I think it's made me jealous
of your success. And I know, I know we've talked about
it, and I'm for feminists. But I don't know. Maybe it's
some deep patriarchal rot left in me. Maybe, given
what's happened, what I've done, I'd feel just as jealous
if I were gay and you were the man I lived with. I can't
separate my ego from its culture very easily. And maybe
not only because you're so good at what you do but
because you're perceived to be good, whereas a good
homicide detective is still and always a corpse cop. Or
because what you do well isn't violent and what I do
gets me more and more crazy since the cocaine bribe.
Yes, and I also very much envy your detective work
because it's not who murdered Monet, who poisoned
Pissarro."

"Who humped Natasha?"

"Karen..."

"Crude, is it? Well, you make me angry and crude. And what you say may be true, but as to the violence and the guilt and the jealousy—you're going to have to work it out if you want us to stay together. And jumping into bed with other women isn't the way. I don't need that sort of signal from you. That's like shooting the driver dead at an intersection rather than using a stop-light."

"Yes. Karen, please let me try."

"Maybe. Maybe. I am so damned hurt and humiliated. I'm not promising anything. But maybe."

He went to the sofa.

"No! Just no touching now. No seductions. Enough seduction."

She flipped open an Italian art book on the coffee table. A man was seated on a chair in front of a blue mountain. The sky was red and the man had the head of an elephant and the head was completely bandaged. It frightened Schwartz. Who was under the bandage? Ginger? Himself? And how different were these two bent cops?

"Oh," he said, wincing. "That cocaine. Oh, that fucking cocaine . . ." He spun around. Jake stood in the doorway.

"Hi, Dad, Mom. I got a lift from New Haven with Terry. What's all this about cocaine?"

4

Jimmy Dee's Cocktail Lounge and Piano Bar is right in the middle of Bridgehampton and its heavy canvas awnings are decorator candy-stripe, which is Cartier ivory and Peck & Peck pink. It has had its ups and its ups, its uppitiest being that Saturday afternoon when Andy *and* Truman *and* Marilyn were said to be in there tipsy together and the traffic was backed solid to Watermill for two hours.

But of the three at the table in the corner farthest from the front window, only Vladimir knows this, not because he is a famous artist but because he is a Russian emigré, and it is now apparent that a Russian emigré, whether butcher or baker or samovar maker, is completely hip to any American social scene not more than fifteen minutes after passing through customs at JFK and being hustled by an illegal taxicab driver, usually someone from Minsk who'd been to Moscow once and says, "New York nice, is nice but, you know, is provincial."

So much so that Vladimir is very comfortable while the other two are squirmy. Ginger is slightly squirmy because this is not his sort of place. His sort of place is darker and woodier and is dedicated to the heterosexual family. In other words, it's generally for men only. On the other hand, here he sits with the famous and wealthy and well born. He only wishes it wasn't so sensationally high profile, though his adverb is earthier. It's not that he feels inferior. Hell no. When he makes it, which won't be long now, he'll be able to *choose* not to come here.

Phil, however, is decidedly squirmy because he knows exactly where he is and fears being seen with a policeman, which is really tacky, and with a policeman who is blackmailing him and who would kill him if he didn't cooperate, which is really tacky and scary.

But Vladimir is not only hip, he is a natural leader and is trying to relax the other two by telling an amusing anecdote. He's describing what passes for a fashionable bar in a millionaire's retirement town he's visited in deepest west Florida. "The kind of a bar," he says, "where three people come in and one asks for a cranberry martini and another asks for a bourbon and vermouth, light on the vermouth, and the third asks for a scotch sour and names the whiskey—and where the bartender nods and mixes them right away, because these are such popular drinks."

Phil understands he should smile and does and sips deep from his neat Glenlivet. Ginger thinks the drinks described are stupid and that anyone who'd drink them must be a jerk, but he senses he can't say that here so he hoists one side of his mouth in a smile that immediately falls back of its own glum weight.

Phil puts down his drink. A man is at the ivory-lacquered piano, but the man isn't Jimmy Dee. Jimmy Dee will only and occasionally play for his very special friends. He's good, Jimmy Dee. He plays a light, open, early boppish piano and sings with a light, open-mouthed voice. He's sometimes called the white Nat

Cole, but less and less these days as he likes it less and less and has become quite plump and wealthy and his spare time is spent raising very large sums of money for the Bide-A-Wee set.

Phil says, "Schwartz knows. Or if not knows, suspects. I can't see how we can go on."

Vladimir looks at Phil and smiles. This is a magnificent smile, imperial and warm at once.

Ginger looks at Phil and sneers with threatening contempt. "Take it from me, Phil—he knows nothing."

Vladimir says, "Yes, do take it from him, Phil. Everything is under control. Simply remain calm and this business will proceed and will be extremely profitable. Leave it to us."

"And take it from me, it's completely legal," Ginger adds, running his finger through the water drops condensed on his three-dollar-and-seventy-five-cent glass of beer that he will, by God, soon be in a position to order without wondering why it should cost so damn much.

Phil doesn't want to, but Phil takes it from them and leaves it to them because they're explaining everything. Phil knows they're explaining nothing because it's in their interest and probably his own for him to remain ignorant, so he swallows his doubts with Glenlivet.

The medley ends. The pianist who isn't Jimmy Dee looks up and in the shallow handclap recognizes Vladimir and asks if he'd like to request a tune, perhaps "Ochi chornye"?

And Vladimir gives him the coolest smile and asks for "Straighten Up and Fly Right."

5

Nothing. Schwartz told Jake the cocaine reference was nothing, a jurisdiction problem with some young detectives in the department. Jake seemed satisfied. Schwartz looked at Karen and Karen looked away.

Jake's one-day visit provided Schwartz a flag of truce beneath which he drew breath and regrouped the scattered pieces of his ego. But it was a gag to Karen, and the relief she felt at its removal, Jake's departure, troubled her.

They stood by the fence waving at the dust until the jeep turned beyond the pines.

"That was nice," he said.

"You should have told him. That would have been the right time, yesterday. He could have coped."

"I couldn't."

They went back in and stayed behind their books. Schwartz didn't read. He thought of the bribe and of Jake, and he knew it wasn't the law's forgiveness or Gallagher's or even Karen's—he'd always had Karen's —but Jake's that he needed to be whole again. But to get Jake's forgiveness he'd have to tell, to confess, the whole awful business to Jake. He couldn't. He couldn't. So he pretended to read and waited for bedtime, when,

as the night before, they'd wear pajamas and curl apart
at the far edges of the bed.

Schwartz knew he wouldn't sleep and fell immediately, furiously asleep.

A bell rang. And again. He sat up and dreamt he
went to the door. Natasha said she couldn't stay away.
They shouldn't evade it like this. He told her he
wasn't evading. He was avoiding her and confronting
it and would she please leave. It was fun and foolish
and over. He knew he was asleep. Back in the bedroom, Karen asked who it was. He said Natasha and
he'd sent her away and Karen said, "Oh," and he
went to sleep.

Schwartz woke sweaty. In the shower he wasn't sure
which bits of last night had been real.

Karen was having coffee by the pool. "Here," she
said. "This was under the door."

He read the note aloud: "I am sorry. I loved you
and wanted to love Karen too. But both of you are
cowards. That is immoral. I won't bother you again.
Natasha."

He looked at Karen. "So I didn't dream it."

"That's not a bad note, as utopian fantasy notes go,
but I'm not a coward. And I wouldn't count on her not
bothering you again." She looked across the pool into
the trees. "Do you want her to?"

"No. I told her there was nothing, it was all over, and
I meant it. I didn't know if I was awake or asleep so I
meant it. That proves it, doesn't it?" He sat down and
put his hand on Karen's arm.

She pulled away. "It doesn't. Some time may." She
shook her head. "I hope some time will."

He said, "Yes." There was something about Jake
he'd wanted to tell her, some ideas he'd had. What? He

couldn't remember. After a while he said, "I'm going to the County Hospital at Riverhead. Two friends of Amboys, very nice old people, had their home . . . their home destroyed to keep them quiet. I don't think it will."

"And who do you think did that—Vladimir?"

"No. But that's just a technicality."

Schwartz was encouraged: Karen's scowl was the warmest look she'd given him for days.

The inland drive was hot. Riverhead baked. The parking lot baked. Heat rose in waves from the macadam and the hoods and roofs and trunks of cars. Hampton heat, Schwartz thought.

Inside, the hospital was too cold. Schwartz sat sneezing by Fran Jansen's bed. The small man sat up; his thin white hair had been brushed down over his forehead like a Dutch boy's, and the brown deep-set eyes were open bright.

"Len, I guess the worst of it was over when I got to know Janny was all right, and ditto for her."

"That's good. I was shocked when I saw . . . It was terrible. Let me explain . . ."

"No need."

"There's a need."

"Hey, Len, I know. We're way ahead of you. Figure someone was listening in when we called you Friday night. Then they did all that to scare us off from telling you anything. Right?"

"Right, you're way ahead." He sneezed. "Did you see any faces?"

"No. Too fast. We were blindfolded and gagged and tied up tight by a couple of pros, sure enough. Maybe two, three at most. Wham, bam, alacazam, and we were trussed like ducks. Heard everything breaking.

That was hard, Len. They didn't say anything. Just kept at it."

"Do you understand how bad it is?"

"The whole kit and caboodle, right?"

"Yes, everything in your beautiful . . . I'm so sorry."

"Sure, sure. But, heck, *we're* okay."

"Do you have insurance?"

"Some, not much. No point, really. Not replaceable, most of that."

Schwartz sneezed and looked down at a very small pair of slippers. In the next bed lay an old man, snoring. His cheeks were bristled white and sunk. His teeth sat in a stainless steel pan on the bed table. Schwartz sneezed again.

"You okay, Len?"

"What? Oh, Jesus. Yes. Sorry, Fran. Fran, can you remember what you were going to tell me about Amboys?"

"Course I can. What do you take me for, a senile old codger like him?" He nodded toward the next bed. "Well, here it is. Jan and I got talking about those last times we saw Vic and remembered what he told us about setting up a meeting to work out what could be done about the Shinnecock deed he'd found. Said one of the Russian painters had put him onto young Phil Troost, that's Rita Troost's boy. Well, suppose he couldn't be that young anymore. About your age. Big man out here in conservation, land use, zoning. That's what Vic said."

"What Russian painter? Yasha Kalubin or one of the Glebor brothers?" asked Schwartz, leaning forward, trying not to leap out of his chair.

"No, wasn't one of them. Was . . . Wait a second, was something like 'Told off.' No . . ."

"Soloff? Was that it?"

"Yup. Soloff. You got it, Len. Well, Vic was real excited. For him, I mean. Thought something might come of him and those two getting together, sort of discussing ways to get that land back to the Shinnecocks. Oh, and we worked out that Vic must have told us that the last time we saw him. 'Bout mid-April."

Schwartz shook his head. Poor old Amboys. "Fran, you've been terrifically helpful. And very brave, though I don't suppose that means much to you."

"Don't know what you're talking about. Hey! Guess the insurance money will get us another phonograph and some records. Right?" He put out his small brown hand to shake and smiled.

"Right," Schwartz said, sneezing, unable to mention the shopping bag of records he set beside the bed as he stood. "Thanks."

"For what?"

"For solving the case."

"Oh, sure. Hey, you be sure to look in on Janny across the hall there. Since this thing happened she's been worried sick about you. Just let her know you're all right. And take care of that cold."

6

"Solved?"

"As good as," he said. He'd leave the tougher question of proof. "Amboys met with Troost and Soloff. I think Whelehan must have been there; I figure Soloff already knew him. Ginger had been dabbling for some time in all sorts of land deals. A very hungry cop."

"Who do you go for now?"

"Troost. He's the most vulnerable or most scared of me."

"Are you telling Gallagher?"

"No. He's back in the city. I think I'll wait till afterward, this time. This will just be preppy old Phil, the pill of the community, and me."

"Is it dangerous?"

"Are you caring again?"

"It it dangerous? I still don't believe you about Vladimir. But is it dangerous?"

"Phil? What's Phil going to do—hit me over the head with bond issues? But I think I'll stay a step ahead of Ginger, for once, and set this up away from home sweet home's tapped phone. Kiss me good-bye?"

"No."

"Oh."

7

Phil wanted to know if it was necessary. It was. But did it have to be today? It had. Then there was a sour acquiescence. But could they meet at the development at, say, half-past three?

They could, and Phil should keep this to himself. He would.

"Sandcastles." Yes, he'd seen the sign on Scuttlehole Road; it had to be very near the Russians' land. It was no doubt another of those disgusting "Sandcastles: A Very Private Estate. Discriminating Acres. An Investment in Grace for Those Few Who Owe Themselves the Elegance."

Schwartz drove, daydreaming. The developers used the advertising agencies and the advertising agencies were full of Yalies wasting good English degrees. Where was all their fine deconstruction theory now? Where were Husserl and Heidegger, Derrida and what's his name? But Jake couldn't end up on Mad Ave buried under development brochures. He wasn't so sure. That's it, Saussure.

He turned off onto a smaller road, following the signs, turned off again and parked by an orange and rubber office block that had a steering wheel in its penthouse because it turned out to be the biggest bulldozer imaginable. Unimaginable. Bulldozer, herd-dozer, whole Chisholm Traildozer.

And look at all the fun it had been having here! Hills had been leveled to lawn sites; thousands of trees had been ripped up and knocked down and dragged out to improve the land for golf courses and green composition tennis courts. Even now great heaps of trees lay, roots sticking from brown orange earth, waiting to be burned. And on every flattened hill and filled-in dale were boundary and foundation markers for the future, little white sticks out of the sandy earth like a fine new cemetery.

And there, not more than a hundred grassless yards in front of Schwartz, the completely nearly finished Model Home and Sales Office stood waiting. And it was everything he'd feared and even less. It was of the de rigueur ersatz, demi-cozy neo-broken-pediment school, New Canaanites become new philistines.

Not, he thought, stepping on the path of sand and nails and slivers of blue plastic, that the aesthetic was the argument. Even if this weren't a steel gray and fey pink grotesquerie, the land would still be stripped, sucked dry, made sterile. . . .

Phil Troost sat busy behind a desk of Chippendale refectory post-modern.

"Chipmonk period?" asked Schwartz, knocking on the inside of the door.

"What? Oh, hello. What? No . . . Oh, I see. Very good. Well, it's the decorator's idea. I'm just going over . . . It's going to be about the finest private community—"

"Yes, I've seen your little bulldozer, but the earth didn't move for me. Phil, I'm not buying a house. I'm here to ask you again if you've told me all you know about Amboys."

Troost looked at Schwartz, looked down, aligned a small pile of papers and moved them to the side. "Yes, I've told you all I know."

"Well, I'm not buying that, either," said Schwartz, sitting down on the pile of papers at the desk edge. "Phil, I'm about to use a very awkward, very ugly word, for which, in these surroundings, I feel bound to apologize in advance. 'Unintimidatable'—that's the word. See, I have it from a very reliable, very unintimidatable source that Victor Amboys had set up a meeting with you last April, mid-April, about the time he was killed. Now, considering he was found at your place . . . Well, Jesus, Phil, I'd hoped it wouldn't come to this, but I'm afraid that makes you my chief suspect."

Troost ran his hand through his blond hair and smiled. "*Your* suspect? But this is a local matter. You have no—"

"Phil." Schwartz held up two fingers, like a priest about to confer a blessing. "Don't tell me about police politics. If I tell the local chief of police you're it, then you're it; he has to go with that. It's not worth the aggravation to him if he didn't. I'm not kidding."

Troost's hand went through his hair again. He didn't smile. He turned his head toward the window, through which was temporary landscaping and pots of daisy trees alternating with pots of geraniums going back up a slope to the next house, an *almost* completely nearly finished one whose facade was all small circle and fake fanlight.

"Could you please?" he said, pointing to the papers under Schwartz.

"What's this, a map of the development?" Schwartz asked, picking a tube of paper from the desk, rolling off its rubber band and spreading it out, still seated on the papers.

Troost made a move for it, but Schwartz motioned him back with a two-fingered wave, pissed off yet pontifical. The lower eighth of the map showed the site they were on: "Sandcastles (First Phase)." The other seven-eighths was labeled "Probable Second through Seventh Phases."

"Oh, cute, all this second-through-seventh stuff up here, Phil, this Russian Art Community land. Have you sold any yet? Is this a subleasing scam? Anyway, with the other evidence, I'd say it was cute enough to get you twenty. You know what twenty is? That's twelve years of hard time. You know what 'hard time' is, don't you, Phil?"

A large motor started up.

"I have nothing to say. My lawyers will deal with any genuine charges, Inspector. As a matter of fact, if you persist with this gangster style of questioning, my lawyers will be dealing with you."

A deep rumbling came from outside.

"'Hard time' means no time off for being very nice, no time off for being well connected. And no country-club jail. Have you ever seen inside the real penitentiaries in this state? Shocking! Dickensian. Hard Times. Oh, and the folks you do your twelve with are . . . Well, they haven't been to Lawrenceville, and they don't know which spoon to use with the prison vichyssoise, and, I might be doing you a gross injustice, but I don't think you'd find them fun."

The office window filled with black and orange. Schwartz watched the giant bulldozer rumble toward the house on the slope. Troost pushed his chair back from the desk and stuck his feet out and put his hands in his pockets and looked bored.

"Very good. You're tougher than I thought. Not so good—you're stupider. I'm here to do you a favor, Phil. And I don't even like you." Schwartz looked out the window. "More landscaping around here?"

"I really don't know. It's a big project, Inspector."

"And if you're not careful, you'll be dying to make it bigger. The bunch of you—what a rum lot! And what rum lots out there."

"Oh, yes, someone told me you'd be witty."

Schwartz got off the desk and went to the window. "I'm not a builder or developer, but, Phil, should that be happening up there?"

With an expression of resigned tedium, Troost came to the window, his hands still in his trouser pockets. A hundred yards beyond, the bulldozer backed away from the corner of the house. Troost's hands popped out of his pockets and gripped the windowsill. The corner of the house was gone. It had been knocked into the house so that the sub-Lutyens roof sagged down and siding and two-by-fours hung bare and split into the dusty gap.

"I'll have your badge for this, Schwartz!" Troost went for the phone.

Schwartz, still looking out the window, said, "Nothing to do with me. Honestly, it's not my style. But I think I recognize whose it is. Are you sure you didn't tell anyone about our meeting? Jesus, Phil, look at that! A third of the house must have come down that time. My guess is that it's either the latest architectural fad—sort of instant New Brutalism—or that you made the mistake of informing Detective Sergeant Whelehan

about our meeting." Schwartz turned. "Ah, yes, the lat-
ter."

Troost stood at the desk with his hand on the phone,
looking out to where the bulldozer rolled up toward the
house front. Schwartz watched, but it was difficult to
see the house behind the big machine. Then the machine
backed off. Now it was difficult to see the house because it mostly wasn't there.

The hand on the phone began to shake. Troost
gripped the receiver hard to still it.

"I think, don't you, that this is Ginger's subtle way
of saying 'Shh, don't say anything, especially the
truth,'" Schwartz said, coming back to the desk. "Sit
down, Phil."

Phil sat.

Schwartz sat back on the pile of papers. "But
Ginger's warning isn't working. I mean, you and I in
here know you're unintimidatable by me—but what
about them? Haven't we been in here for long enough
so that they'll think you're spilling out your blond
boyish guts to me? Yes. You know, I can understand
them, Whelehan and his rent-a-thug. What I can't figure is why you keep hanging in there with them.
They're finished for certain as business associates, and
I can't imagine you'd want them as friends. What?"

Troost was pointing to the window. The bulldozer
was coming back down the slope. Troost's mouth hung
open a bit; it wasn't becoming.

"Hmm. I think so, Phil. I think they're hard
enough."

The earthmover blocked the light off from the window as it passed. It turned the corner to the front of the
Model House.

"Do something! For Christ's sake, you're the law. Do something, stop them! Inspector, please!"

"Ah. Now that's tricky. No, sit down, Phil. I really have to insist you stay seated." Schwartz lifted his arm so that his loose shirt pulled tight and Troost could see the bulge of the holster.

"I was saying it's tricky. In the first place, those gentlemen out there are your friends, not mine—your invited guests. And, as you point out, this isn't really my jurisdiction. And then there's the sacredness of private property, and this is *your* private property. So, although I appreciate your problem, old sport, my hands are—"

Schwartz fell off the desk. Plaster fell on his head and powdered around him. He shook it from his hair and flicked plaster from the shoulders of his shirt. He stood, sat back on the skewed desk and asked, "Are you okay?"

Troost remained in the chair, completely in the chair, his legs raised onto it, his arms around his knees, curled as if for birth, an air crash or mound burial. He said, "Please."

Schwartz patted the holster. "Well, what can I tell you, Phil? I suppose twice more, the way you've pitched your mansion. Yes, at most two more taps on the door from Leviathan out there before the place is flattened. Personally, I'd rather have a late afternoon swim out at the beach."

They heard the machine back off.

"I like this time of day for a swim: the water calm, the beach almost empty, and there's a certain slant of light—"

"All right," said Troost. His hands unclasped and flapped over his knees; his blue blazer was flaked white;

a small wedge of plaster stuck in front of his hair. "It's true that I'm in with them, but I didn't . . . It's a long story—"

"And a gripping one, too, I'll bet, but we don't have the budget for a feature. One short scene—Amboys out at your place, his final minutes."

"Right. He was . . . Jesus, that thing's coming again!"

"Keep talking, Phil," Schwartz said, bracing himself.

"Amboys was going to meet us, Vladimir and me, at my place. But neither had shown up. I was only intending to convince him there was no chance the Indians could ever get—"

Troost and the chair disappeared as Schwartz and the desk lifted off and thudded back in a tearing sound which was the moving of the wall behind him. Schwartz squeezed his eyes shut.

The ceiling came down, but it was too late to dive beneath the desk. Heavy plaster broke on Schwartz and in the sharp thwack of the two-by-four or more across his shoulder, he felt pleased that it missed his head. He opened his eyes to dust in daylight. He was, somehow, still on the edge of the desk. "Phil?"

"Oh, please, oh, Jesus, please let's get out of here," came the voice from behind and below the desk.

Schwartz leaned over. The chair had fallen back into a hole in the floor so that Troost was tipped into it with his feet up under the desk. Its middle drawer, filled with plaster, was in his lap.

Schwartz reached down; Troost took his hand and pulled. Schwartz pushed back. "Finish your story."

"We'll be buried alive, killed!"

"Phil."

"You shit. If you didn't have that gun, you bastard

. . . Okay, Okay. They were an hour late and I was looking for them out on the beach porch when I saw
Amboys coming up between Soloff and Whelehan. I
didn't even know what Whelehan was doing there. I'd
met him and knew he was involved with some developers, but that's all. They were shouting, but I couldn't
make it out in the wind and rain. And then I saw . . . I
swear I'm telling you the truth. I saw a gun in Whelehan's hand and he started beating Amboys over the head
with it, like with the butt. Over and over. It was terrible,
and so I ran down to stop him but it was too late.
Amboys was on the ground dead and they scared me
into shutting up and helping to bury him. I mean, with
Whelehan being a policeman. Look, I admit I was stupid and scared but I swear I had nothing to do with
killing him. Please? Please can we please get out of
here?"

Troost was pulling at his hand. Schwartz listened.
The bulldozer was far off from the house and seemed to
be idling.

"We're almost ready, Phil. Just try to remember. Did
you see Amboys walking on the beach or up the dunes
with the other two?"

"Yes. Well, I think so. It was dark and raining. They
were close together, one on either side of Amboys like
they might have been forcing him to walk along. That's
what I saw. Please."

"And the deed?"

"I never . . . Wait, no, Whelehan went through his
pockets and found it and said he'd take care of it. And
that's the last I saw of it. Please! We're going to be
killed in here. Whelehan's crazy!"

"Oh, that won't be him at the wheel out there.
Ginger's a cruel man but not stupid." Schwartz pulled

Troost's hand and helped him up. Then he picked the piece of plaster from Troost's hair.

"No, Phil, I don't think these places are so well built. The hollow walls, for instance, and the floors. They look nice, but—"

The bulldozer appeared out the still-intact window at the side of the house. Schwartz nodded and Troost stepped away over the rubble onto the sun deck that had been the front hall.

Schwartz didn't like it, but he stood in the window. The bulldozer started forward. Schwartz shrugged and pulled the pistol from its holster. He felt his sweat on the leather. He picked up a piece of floorboard, but maybe he wouldn't have to break the window. The bulldozer stopped. Funny, how even in a wrecked house he'd feel like a vandal if he had to break a window.

"Phil, be safe and stay where you are. I'm going out."

He stepped past Troost, who crouched under a doorframe that led from outside to outside.

Everything was still. Obviously, whoever was up there was doing some thinking about the wisdom of killing a cop. But he'd come to a decision: a bullet hit the corner of the house and Schwartz ducked back.

It was time for strategic withdrawal, reinforcements, that sort of . . . By walking through the wrecked house he could get around the corner. Schwartz crawled along the back of a sofa upholstered in wall. There, through that gap, oh, yes, hooded, too, he was, sliding out of the cab.

"Throw down your gun! You're surrounded by police," yelled Schwartz, embarrassed by his hokey lie.

But it was, Jesus, it was working. The hooded hood

was looking down at his gun, then holding it out butt first and . . .

He fell off the bulldozer in the gunshot.

Schwartz backed from the sofa, saw he couldn't get through the gap in the wall and ran back through the house. A second shot. Of course. The bastard would make sure.

The bastard stood over the body at the base of the two story machine. He was still two steps ahead.

Schwartz walked up to him. "What a surprise! Gee, thanks."

~~~~~ 8

"**J**ust doing my job. Phil called me because he was worried you might be violent. He told me there'd been some trouble with you like that already, at his club. So, of course, I thought I'd better come out, seeing the sort of trouble that seems to follow you. And looks like I arrived just in time. This man was shooting at you."

"Yeah, Ginger. Just in time. Or maybe a little too late. Phil and I have had an interesting talk. You're good, though, Ginger. Jesus, you would have made a good officer of the law if you didn't spend all your time breaking it."

"Sir?" asked Whelehan, slipping into formal incomprehension.

"That second shot, the one through the head as this poor shit lay wounded on the ground. Some coup de grace. And when he's identified as a criminal you've had dealings with, you'll survive that too—with a little help from your department friends. You know, I can see why they don't like me, but I'm damned if I know why they like you so much."

For a second, a smile thought of showing up on Whelehan's face.

"Ginger, here comes Phil," said Schwartz, stopping his hand as it crossed to put the gun in the holster. "If you even blink as if you mightn't recognize him and go for your gun, if you even think . . . But no. You're way too smart for that. You need to stay alive to become rich and party with the big boys."

Whelehan shook his head sadly, pityingly. "I just want your statement and Phil's as to what was happening here, either now or later at the station."

Troost, powdery and shaken, stopped half behind Schwartz and stared at the corpse.

"Phil, see how your partner finished this one—another of his partners? Look at the gun over there, fifteen feet away. Some self-defense, that second shot. What was his threat, Ginger—to drown you in his own blood?"

Troost kept staring at the body. The blood that showed red was on the ground under the head. The rest was a wet stain on the sweatshirt and the wetness soaking down the tight black hood.

Troost looked up, still keeping behind Schwartz. "Ginger, I've told Inspector Schwartz what happened. I mean with Amboys that night on the beach. I had to. You see, he—"

"I understand, Phil. Of course you had to. And I'm sure when we have your full statement—the whole truth of the circumstances under which you told the inspector whatever you did—he'll be the first to agree that it's not evidence. It could never be used in any court."

Troost looked at Schwartz. Schwartz heard the sirens coming up the road. Great timing. Well, it certainly was Ginger's home ground. "You're right, Ginger. I've messed up. I seem to be getting worse and worse on procedure, especially on the away games. I think I'll have to change my offense."

Whelehan shook his head. "You have me all wrong."

"No, partly wrong. I've seriously underestimated you."

The sirens grew very loud, stopped, doors slammed and a lieutenant joined them. "What's happened?"

Whelehan deferred to Schwartz.

"What you have here," said Schwartz, nodding toward the dead man, "is a critic of contemporary architecture."

"What?"

Schwartz looked back to the house. "A deconstructionist. Thank you for your confession, Phil. I hope you'll stick to it, on quiet reflection. I'll get back to you. Ginger, may I have a word?"

They walked away from Phil, who was now crouching, and from the lieutenant, who was telling him to take deep breaths and stop looking at the corpse.

"Ginger, I'd like to give you my statement personally."

"Fine."

"At your house?"

Whelehan blinked a few times. "Why not, if it saves you from breaking in. Anyhow, I could use a complete statement on this. You know the red tape, how the shit flies every time you fire a shot. When should we meet?"

"What about now?"

"Sure, if I can clear it with the lieutenant."

If he can clear it . . . Schwartz stood pushing a furrow in the sand with the toe of his sneaker. Whelehan could clear the invasion of New Jersey with this bunch. And why is he so agreeable? And how is it I'm so crappy a cop and this hustling, bent Whelehan is going to get away with murder—two of them?

Whelehan walked back. "It's all clear; we can go. Oh, watch it, Len. Your foot's in a sand hole."

―――――― 9

When he'd answered that, yes, he knew the address, Whelehan had driven off. Without a smile, a sneer or snippet of surprise, Schwartz hissed to himself as he stood at the pump putting gas into the car. Why, Detective? Why? Because he wants you to go there? Why? Because what's there isn't what you expect. But what do I ex—"Oh, shit!"

The gas ran out onto his sneaker. He shook it,

vaguely, paid and wondered how long the Hamptons gas stations would remain havens of reality before for every hundred gallons or ten quarts of Quaker State you got your free Hermès scarf?

Whelehan's house was definitely not in South-hampton's *quartier* Hermès. In the northeast of town, it was on a street of small wooden and stuccoed houses built in the twenties. These were very seriously clean houses on tiny raised plots heavily surrounded with evergreens that signaled "We're ordinary people as good as you are and we *choose* not to smile very much."

"Come in, the door's open. Want a beer?" Ginger's voice called pleasantly.

Schwartz stood on the tiny veranda looking at its stubby columns of the Sears order dork-doric. "No, thanks," he said, entering and turning as Ginger pointed into the living room—no, definitely a sitting room—where he understood why he was so welcome.

It was small and paneled in stained plywood with darker brown stripping at the borders, turns and shelf ends. Too shallow for books, these shelves seemed made for the photos and trophies which covered all four walls. And, oh, my, wasn't this a nifty shrine to self. Ginger the high school halfback, Ginger the captain of the police pistol club, Ginger with—ah, yes—some local Fords and Onassi, accepting charity checks. There was even an early Ginger, the cherubic choirboy, not quite a Della Robbia, but not bad.

"Sorry, Len. I grabbed a beer for myself. Anything you're looking for in particular?"

"Aside from the one of you and Kissinger sharing the Nobel Peace Prize, no. Oh, this one's touching."

"Yeah, poor kids. I help organize the police picnics

for the crippled children's summer home out here."

"And a big shot in the PBA. Quite something."

"I guess my uncle didn't tell you. Have you stepped in gasoline?"

Schwartz turned from the wall. "Yes. Sorry for the smell. No, Tom didn't say. He really hasn't told me a thing about you."

"I guess that's the best I could hope for. He doesn't like me much. I don't know why. I like him."

"Yeah, sometimes I like him too. So, all right. Okay. You win; you beat me into putting it directly. Why, Ginger? Why? You have a nice life, according to all this. For sure you could have had a great police career. So, not to put it any stronger, why do you hustle around the big land development money out here? It's bound to compromise you."

Ginger nodded into the glass he carefully poured from the bottle. "All right," he said. He took two wooden coasters from the side table, placed the bottle on one and the glass on the other and sat in the armchair across from Schwartz.

"There used to be other pictures in here. Lots. Of myself and my wife, my ex-wife, Jean. This was her folks' house; they left it to her. And when we split up, since she didn't want to stay around here, I bought it off her. Four years ago. Well, when we married, Jean's mother was still alive. Her father had died—of drink, really, when Jean was thirteen or fourteen. He was a local small-timer—handyman, sometimes working in shops. Once even a fireman, but I gather something happened. Anyway, Eleanor, Jean's mother, she was something else. Born a Bonham, one of the big old families out here. And Jean was brought up by her mother to feel that they'd been cheated." Whelehan paused, lifted the beer glass and looked across at Schwartz.

"Yes," Schwartz said. "I don't know the people, but I know this kind of story."

"But the story is that Eleanor was once very in love with Jimmy, Jean's father. They eloped, the family cut her off. All that, you know. Years later, they did get invited around, Jimmy too, but by then she couldn't stand it, and he never could. Well, so her mother put it into her that Jean should want to get that sort of life back. Really, Len, I have to say that I blame the divorce on that old bitch. Sorry, but there it is. So then Jean falls for me, and it was sort of like a repeat of her mother. You know, first year or so we were...it was...Yeah. So then it wasn't enough for her to be a cop's wife. And I was doing well. You see. She wanted...That bitch wanted...Sorry. Anyhow, at least we didn't have kids. So we broke up. But the funny thing was that from then, from after she was gone, I decided I'd show her and all those rich snobs here that I was good enough to make it. I mean, I guess I decided to show myself." He stopped and drank the beer and set the glass back on the coaster and slid the coaster to the middle of the side table.

"You want to tell me anything else?"

"Yes, I do. I admit I was very wrong to put you under observation and take those videos. And it wasn't just personal. You've got one angry police force out here. And, sure, I wasn't going to let you spoil my plans. They're legal, Len. That's all. Everyone sails a bit close to make it. You know that. And I don't want to be a policeman forever, though for as long as I am, I'll be the best I can. So I find I have a flair for property

development. And now I can make it big: Phil Troost's
development is the way. Look, look. These things don't
happen twice. When the chance comes you've got to go
with it or you lose it. No disrespect, but I don't have old
Harvard buddies to help out. So after this, I think I can
get into the business full-time, and then I'll resign from
the force. . . . Well?"

"I have to go home now; I'm smelling up your house
with this sneaker. If you give me the statement sheet,
I'll fill it in myself. I guess one cop can do that for
another."

"Yes, but what I've told you?"

"I've heard it and it's believable. But I also have to
believe my senses: the little house shakedown back
there at Sandcastles, the driver taking a shot at me but
then deciding to give it up—but not fast enough to keep
you from shooting him dead. That's not good procedure, and I see how good a cop you can be. Well, with
your department behind you, and if the driver's record is
bad enough, maybe it'll wash. But then there's the
trashing of the Jansen home. Oh, and even if that wasn't
you—if anything else *seems* to happen to them, I
promise I'll overcome my real dislike for guns for
long enough to drop by and kill you. And I'm saying
this, Ginger, because the Jansens have recalled some
very interesting details told them by their late friend
Amboys. And last but not least there's Victor Amboys
and your really feeble case against that poor Indian kid.
So, all in all, I don't know, Ginger; so much seems to
be pointing your way. And that's not considering your
famous buddy Soloff."

"I see," said Whelehan, standing. "Wait a second.
I'll get the statement sheets."

A very scary second, Schwartz thought. He's either

going to come back with his trusty .38 pointed between
my eyes or . . .

"Take that," said Ginger, handing him the form. "I'm
sorry you still suspect me. You're wrong, but thanks for
at least putting all your cards on the table."

"I'll get this in tomorrow or the next day," Schwartz
said, walking past Ginger's outstretched hand.

He turned at the bottom of the steps. "Ginger, just so
we're clear: I put *some* cards on the table. I've still got a
few in the hole."

Ginger nodded and closed the screen door, and
Schwartz forgave himself the trite good-bye as he
thought of the photos he'd found of Jean, the ones used
in the divorce proceedings. Nice Detective Whelehan
was one mean killer.

~~~~~ **10**

It was hot at six-thirty when he got home, or not home
but to this slick white gallery. He looked at the statement form and dropped it onto the white marble table.
Maybe he and Karen could go out for a quiet swim back
in the bay, at Fresh Pond.

He heard her typing as he read the note on the study
door: "Working until at least 7:30. Don't disturb.
Thanks, K."

He looked at the pool. He should shower. He should take off the fuming sneaker. He made a large gin and tonic and was slicing the lime when he remembered. He poured it into the sink.

He looked at his cassettes; he could play one low enough so that Karen . . .

Well, there was *Karamazov* to reread, but the last time he'd tried that he'd heard his father's voice heavy with sarcasm: "You slay me." And why did he associate that tone with pickled herring?

He opened the fridge and saw he wasn't hungry.

So he sighed and did what he should have done first. When they told him Deputy Chief of Detectives Gallagher wasn't there, he had the call switched to his own office and asked a voice he didn't recognize to put him through to Detective Captain Malinowski who was there and who spoke for twenty minutes about how bad a job he was doing deputizing so that Schwartz had to ask for details and found, as he knew he would, that Bob was doing a perfect job and told him so, upon which Bob became near fluttery with the praise and said he'd heard of some of Schwartz's exploits out on the island.

Schwartz heard himself say, "Exploits? Exploits? God, has it gotten to exploits?" But he couldn't bring himself to explain the link between his failures and bad prose, and he had an image of certain balletic exploits Natasha had bent him to, and, confused, he thanked Bob, promised he'd be in touch and said he'd be back right after Labor Day.

But it was only seven and the typing clicked on steadily from behind the door, so he dialed Riverdale.

"Yeah?"

"Hello. This is Len, Tom."

"Lenny, what's up?"

"Nothing much, considering what's happened. I got a complete confession from Phil Troost. He saw Ginger beat Amboys to death with the butt of his gun. And considering the circumstances under which I got the confession, with which I'll delight and terrify you some other time, I'm sure Master Phil was telling the truth."

"So that wraps it up?"

"No. For one thing, as your nephew briskly pointed out, those same circumstances pretty much invalidate the confession. But even if my methods were above board, that confession pretty well clears Ginger of the murder."

"Lenny, Lenny, we're just about to sit down to a pot roast dinner. You've had Kitty's pot roast, so you know. I'll listen to what's important, but I'm asking you to tell it like you're talking on the phone to your hungry boss, not like a contestant in the Phil Silvers competition."

"Yes, boss. Here's the potted version. The coroner's report states the cause of death most probably to be from one immense break in the skull itself. There are additional smaller cracks, contusions, whatever. I've seen the photos and the big bang theory must be right. It's like a tree fell on Amboys."

"Yeah. And?"

"So either someone or something got him with a log or a whatever—but before Troost saw him. Soloff and Whelehan brought Amboys along to Troost's, but I'm pretty sure they were holding up a corpse. And then they staged an argument and fake killing in front of Troost."

"Oh, I see—to get Troost thinking he was so implicated that he'd have to go along with them."

"Exactly, young fellow. Have you considered a career in the police force?"

"Listen, that's something. Even if Ginger didn't kill him, you can't go around mauling stiffs."

"Yes, Tom, but that's small stuff."

"Yeah, but if that's all you've got—"

"No, it's not." Schwartz turned to see Karen sit on the arm of the sofa. "I have another piece of frustration. When Troost told Whelehan, despite my warning, that he was going to see me, your sweet nephew sent in a goon on a giant earthmover to scare Troost quiet. And then Ginger arrived in the nick of time to save himself by shooting his hireling very dead, on the pretense that he was helping save me. And that's a murder he's going to get away with. And...Jesus, I hate telling a great story so flatly, but I can smell your pot roast."

"Any other cops around?"

"Sure. Just late enough. And my bet is they'll give Ginger some paid time off duty for bad behavior, but nothing so drastic as a temporary suspension pending investigation. What do you think, Uncle Thomas?"

"I ain't protecting him! He's no favorite, I promise you. I never liked the jerk my sister Patty married. She's got a couple of nice girls, but Ginger takes after Dick—Dick in name and dick in deed."

"Chief?"

"Yeah?"

"Stop clowning. You have a serious pot roast to attend to. Let me just say that after having a nice talk with Ginger in his nice house with all his nice trophies and photos attesting to his niceness, I came away a bit sickened—especially by his nice story about his marriage and divorce. I don't want to pry, Tom, but I have seen some of that evidence Jean presented to that sexist old fart judge in order to get a bit of help in the divorce. Battery? She was lucky to get away alive. And he's our man, if we can get him."

"Yeah. I should have told you about Jean. But, Jesus, we are all so ashamed of that."

"Okay, okay. I understand. I'll think of something. Are you coming out here soon?"

"Probably not. It doesn't look like I can make it out there now until just before Labor Day weekend, for that end-of-the-season bash we're giving. So stay in touch on this. You going to try getting some corroboration from that Russian painter?"

"I guess. Oh, not that it matters, but is my line still tapped?"

"I don't know."

"I hear you, Thomas. Bye."

He looked across at Karen. "Is that concern?"

"I picked up some of that. What's happened?"

"Plenty. Maybe Amboys wasn't exactly murdered, but there sure as hell's a murderer loose and—"

"But it's not Vladimir."

"No. No, I'm sorry to say the killer has a badge and a gun and a grudge."

"Oh. Against you?"

Schwartz nodded.

"Yes. Well, in that case, I'm concerned."

"Ah, you do care."

"You misunderstand me. I'm concerned that I'm in danger. Am I?"

Karen's voice sounded flatter than Schwartz found tolerably ironic or even tolerable. "Yes," he said. "I think so. He sounds very flaky when referring to women." He paused, thinking of Ginger in his little tree house with Karen in his lens. "We can get a few plainclothes police, women if you wish, if you want to stick around. Or, safer, you could clear out back to the city."

"'Clear out' sounds best. But not to the city."

"Oh? Then to where?" he asked, knowing.

"Baldock Island. The Manor House. I have work to do. And don't tell me it won't be safe. Vladimir is a painter; his politics may be reactionary, but he's not a cop or any other sort of thug. And, frankly, these days it's around *you* that I don't feel safe."

"Charming. Well, now you can't accuse me of unconsciously using you for bait, like on that case last spring. You'll be setting yourself up, and all up front."

"'Up front.' God, you sound like some cheap..."

He waited, but she didn't go on. "Cop? Isn't that what you were going to say? Cheap cop rather than fancy art-book publisher or famous fascist painter?"

"No. Just cheap cop," Karen said, standing. "Of course you used me last spring. But I never said a word about it until now. That was your own guilt." Her mouth pulled down as if she'd eaten lemon. "You know, I'd just begun to work well here. I just had a good chapter going in there. And then you... You have to, you find something from your slimy life to screw me up."

"Karen, be reasonable. It's my professional opinion that there are two men out there who are very dangerous to us. And it's my professional, not to mention moral, obligation to protect us both. But I can't imprison you to do it."

"Leonard, I think I liked the cheap cop better than this pompous cop."

Schwartz sank back into the armchair and put his

head down. His shirt stank worse than his sneaker. "Do what you want."

He sat there hot and smelly. He was a cheap cop. He was a pompous cop. He heard Karen packing in the bedroom.

She came out. "I'm going to the island for my own work, for my *own* protection. And if you think that gives you license to start up with that wide-eyed siren of the steppes or anyone else, you're a very stupid cop."

He heard the car start and drive off. Okay, he was a cheap and pompous and stupid cop, but he was hot and smelly and tired and all he'd wanted was to go swimming out at Fresh Pond with his wife, and how had all this happened?

Very well. No panic. He'd put on—yes, why not—some sparkle: Chopin mazurkas. Yes, a little swim in Chopin and then one in the bay. And he wondered, since it had been Karen's choice to go to the island, damn it, how he just might use his darling wife to get those killers.

BOOK IV

1

The bay in the evening cooled but didn't soothe him. The beach which should have been serene was marred by sand fleas and the line of Baldock Island, dim, northeast. Soloff—what he had to do was get to Soloff. The Volvo had filled with Fresh Pond mosquitoes that hitched to him—forearm, back of neck and ankle— halfway to Amagansett, where he was able to gun the car and blow them away.

Soloff—but first he'd shower and then he'd barbecue a steak. He damn well would enjoy his own company. Karen was acting crazy, that was all. What were his fears for her but stupid projections of his own insecurities? And Whelehan might be unpredictable, but he was interested in saving his neck to save his deal; threatening Karen wouldn't help. And Soloff . . . But now that he'd shaved and showered, he'd grill a steak.

Listen to that mazurka, as much Rubinstein's as Chopin's. Dum DUM ta-da, dum DUM ta-da. And what could Soloff gain from Karen? Karen was acting crazy.

What he loved was how the mazurkas were like waltzes but wilder, like the chrysalis of bop cocooned in three/four time. He spread charcoal over the lava stones on the outdoor gas grill—the fuss you had to make to imitate simplicity. Natasha. Was she acting on her own

or still for Soloff? He washed his hands and poured a
V8 on the rocks and sat by the pool waiting for the
perfect short blue flame. If he called Natasha and asked
what Soloff might do, would she answer honestly? Was
she so enamored of abilities? He meant vulnerabilities.
He'd always liked himself in white trousers and bare
feet; he had nice ankles. Karen said they were as good
as hers. Karen was acting crazy, flipped out. His ankles
were lumpy with mosquito bites.

He flipped the steak and then the cassette. It was on
this side, that strange dissonant mazurka that big Art
made sound like Schoenberg, the way Glenn Gould
made that Bach Goldberg sound like Chopin. No funny
business; he'd ask her directly about Soloff. He tossed
the salad and ate it with his steak. Were they a woman's
ankles? Is that what Karen meant? He arched them. Yes,
they could be. He liked the idea. No funny business. He
was having a nice time on his own.

He dropped the fork and knife into their trays and
closed the drawer. It would be a straight question. Either way she answered, he'd learn something. But if the
phone was still tapped by Brennan and Whelehan was
still into Brennan's tap and into Soloff's confidence and
Soloff was trying to get into Karen, into Karen's confidence, would Karen hear of this call to Natasha he
hadn't yet made? And could the phone be bugged, as
well as tapped?

Inside the telephone the wires were coated many
colors. Here was an electric blue like the sail of a Portu-
guese man-o'-war. Or the strings of stingers? No, that
was more this purple wire, which also looked untam-
pered with. The screwdriver was way too large. If he
put it back now . . . At least he hadn't damaged it. He
closed the case and replugged it.

It whirred with a faint, metallic ping-pang.

"Hello?"

"Ln fr pzz tbdd md 11?"

"What? Wait, I'll go to another phone."

"Pnn tb gg f tss n bl?"

"No, another phone. Wait."

But whoever it was had hung up. Had it been Karen? There was a touch of Karen's wit in that "tbdd md." Yet it was Natasha's wistfulness in "gg f."

He knew just the place.

As he drove he saw the lights on through the trees.

He parked. He could call from here, as well, after he'd asked—

"Who is?"

"Len Schwartz, Madame Kalubin. We met—"

"Of course, of course. Lyenny. Is so good to see you. Please, please come in and you must call me Anna. You not perhaps remembering?"

"Yes. No. Thank you," he said to the smile and bone china hands offered his way.

"In here. Come. Yasha will be happy to see you. He remembers how much you drink and dance."

"Ah, yes. I wanted to speak to you about . . . "

It was Natasha in the studio-living room, behind an easel with her grandfather. They were talking; she hadn't looked up. Schwartz couldn't get a certain video moment out of his head.

She looked. "Oh. Len, hi. Hello. Yashinka, look, it's Len."

The old man put his lumped bald head forward and peered. "Len? I not see well so far. Len, you want vodka? I should put on music and you dance?"

"Pas ce soir, maître," Schwartz said, giving a low bow and feeling the blood rush to his face and practi-

cally every other part of him. He shook Yasha's hand
and then looked at Natasha and, as she did, backed off a
step. Could she know about those videos? Had she, oh
damn it, had she helped set them up? Director Whelehan was saying, "Now, Natasha baby, in the poolside
scene I'm going to zoom in . . . "

He said, "Uh . . . "

She said, "If you'd rather, I can go on home now."

"No. I hadn't . . . I'd thought to call you from here,
after I spoke with your grandparents. What are you
working on? May I see?"

"Certainly," the old man said, smiling, with a small
returning bow.

Natasha said, "Oh, but it's not finished. It needs a lot
more work."

Schwartz was looking at an oil painting of a man's
torso, a dark man in a white T-shirt. He looked crazy.
Or not quite. But the look of pain and defensive irony
and the way the dark uncombed hair . . . It was, god, it
was him! After recognition, he thought, a formal feeling
comes—along with an excruciating silence.

"Come, Lyenny," said Anushka, "you help me bring
something out for tea."

In the kitchen he said, "I didn't mean to be rude. But
first Natasha and then that painting. It was a shock. It's
a terrible, wonderful painting. She . . . "

"Please reach for me that can, Lyenny, there. I tell
you something though maybe is none of my business.
We are not all of us like Helen, Natasha's mother. She is
kind daughter-in-law and I love her, but too impulsive
and too sentimental and I know she makes with this
trouble." She was arranging apricots and peaches and
grapes on a platter.

"Do you . . . I don't know if I can ask this without

offending you." He sliced the honey cake she set before him. "Do you know if Soloff asked Natasha to . . . to visit me, that first time?"

"This offends me, yes, but is true. Vladimir has too much power here. Yes, he ask her. He hope . . . But you know it does not happen so. Natasha begin with you as maybe little adventure, but then she change her feeling for Vladimir and like you very much. What 'like'? She love you. You know, you see this painting she make of you. This is not painting from someone who only play or use you. Isn't so?" Anna set the honey cake on the tray with the fruit.

"I can't continue . . . " he began.

"Yes, I know. I am sorry this started, but is Natasha's fault as much. But Natasha," Anna sighed and smiled. "Such a grandchild. She is closest now in many ways to us of whole famuly! Here, you like this? Is mandel bread. You like mandel bread? I learn make this two hundred years ago from Yasha's mother so she didn't think her daughter-in-law such total shiksa."

Schwartz put a piece in his mouth. It crumbled, buttery and walnut. Heaven. "Wonderful."

"Is supposed almonds, but I put always walnut. We have enough?"

He looked at the two large trays of honey cakes and marble cakes and mandel bread and poppyseed cookies and fruit and black bread and butter and jam and said yes. And he took her hand and kissed it and said thank you.

On their way to the living room she turned: "You should believe Natasha. She is good person. She tell us immediately about the poor murdered man and land is maybe for poor Indians and we," she said, making a small circle with her finger, "want only what is right."

The round table was covered with embroidered

flower shawls. The samovar steamed in the middle. Schwartz pulled up his chair so that his back was to the easel, but there was still Natasha to face, sitting across from him.

Yasha kept offering vodka and winked when Schwartz refused. After the old man had taken one himself, Anna tapped her spoon against her plate and he pushed the decanter away and stuck to glasses of lemon tea.

They talked about music and painting, and only when the talk came around to the business of the land and his own involvement did Schwartz look directly at Natasha. He saw her hurt and tender and knew she loved him; and when he knew this he knew the affair was over. He couldn't hurt her by continuing; he couldn't hurt Karen like that. He didn't love Natasha; he loved Karen.

Now he could feel sorry for Natasha. His heart lightened; he felt like a shit. Then his head cleared and he knew he was a fool; his guilt, somehow centered in his groin, had led him in circles. The way of knowing Natasha's game was to let her play it. And if it led back to Soloff, so be it.

"Natasha," he asked, "do you think Karen might be in any physical danger from Vladimir, now that I've spoiled his get-rich plans?"

She looked down. "No, not at all. He's not like that. And he likes Karen, you know, and he's too dedicated to painting and his silly Community of Real Russia plans to do anything that would compromise them."

It was convincing and it wasn't convincing. So he talked and laughed with Anna and Yasha, and when Natasha relaxed and joined in, he invited her to go clamming with him the next morning.

As she nodded yes, he heard her grandmother give a small sigh.

~~~~~~~~ **2**

Even with his eyes shut, Soloff knew someone was standing near his bed. It wasn't her. He would have sensed if it were her. If he let his arm drop over the edge, the iron pipe would be within . . .

"Don't bother, Vladimir."

He opened his eyes to Whelehan. "How did you get in here?"

"I have my ways. As a matter of fact, I probably know more about this island than you do."

"And to what do I owe this visit, beyond your need to show off?"

Ginger pulled a chair to the bedside and sat down. "Don't get snotty with me, big man. Your unsuccessful poisoning tipped Schwartz to the whole business."

"How many times must I tell you: I did not intend—"

"Great. Stick to your story. Listen, I didn't want to use the phone and now . . ."

Soloff had swung his legs off the bed so that his back

was turned on Whelehan. Then he stood, wiry, bare chested in white pajama bottoms, stretched and slowly turned back toward him. "Yes, Ginger, and now—I know about now. Troost called and told me of your asinine bungling at Sandcastles. I think you've finally managed to lose him. And if he's lost, so is the entire project. What is it that possesses you? The mindless, degenerate violence of these television programs and movies of yours?"

"Shut up. Yesterday was nothing. It was time to scare Troost, again. Schwartz can't prove anything and he sure as hell can't use whatever he got from Phil. I figured Troost would call you in his panic and I figured that would panic you. That's why I came over. To reassure you that the deal's still on and it's still good."

Soloff shook his head. "I worry about you, Ginger. We all take risks, but I take them for high ideals, while you . . . Greed will not see you through this, Ginger. It makes—"

"Spare me the Russian priest sermons, will you? Shit. Look at this place. You've got a *studio* here three times the size of my whole house! Ideals, shit. If you want to know, that community place you go on about sounds as bad as the other one, the Russia you left. So let's just keep out of each other's motives, Soloff, okay?"

"Certainly."

"You're damn right, certainly. Now listen—I can take care of my uncle on this thing and Phil will do whatever we tell him, so it's only Schwartz we have to get off our backs. But we really have to do that soon. Our very big silent partner is getting nervous. Any information about Schwartz these days?"

Soloff walked over to an unfinished portrait, backed away and went to the wall, where he drew the curtains. Then he moved slowly toward the easel.

"Hey, genius! I'm talking to you!"

"As a matter of fact, I've learned he's taking Natasha out clamming later this morning. I don't know where."

"She tell you that?"

"Never mind my source. It's true enough."

Whelehan joined Soloff before the easel. "Hey," he said, "that's his wife, Karen, isn't it. Pretty good. You banging her?"

Soloff tensed: "Ginger—Officer Whelehan, you are, in the inimitably vibrant argot of your country, a creep."

Ginger's eyelids dropped. Then he smiled. "Sure, sure. The necessary creep. Well, I think I'll just creep back across the bay and take care of your—*sitter's* husband so that you and Phil and our important friend can keep your talented, well-connected fingers clean."

"Yes. Do that. Spare me the details, but see that you do it properly. Oh, and please don't let anyone here see you on your way out."

"Don't worry," Ginger said, his smile flattening. "They wouldn't see me here if I walked right in front of them. But, Soloff, remember—when it comes down to it, this is *my* show. Right?"

"Yours, of course." Soloff nodded as the door closed. And half under his breath he added, "Idiotic little parvenu."

The door opened again. "I heard that and I understand it. Not bad, huh, a parvenu being able to understand a charismatic asshole. I'll be in touch," said Ginger, closing the door without a sound.

3

Big white clouds lay piled to the south of them. The sun beat down.

"I can't feel anything."

Schwartz turned. "Move it forward, then back."

"But I'm getting sore," Natasha said.

"That's because it's going in too far. Wait."

Schwartz waded back, the basket in the inner tube tugging on the line around his waist. Natasha leaned on her clam rake in a wet T-shirt that he tried not to see he saw through.

"I thought you said it was easy."

"It is. Look." He stuck his rake in so that its handle swayed over the water and put his arms around Natasha from behind. She'd cut her hair shorter; the water shone through it like honey in the sun an inch in front of his mouth.

He drew his head back. "Lightly, push the rake forward lightly over the sand. Hold the handle just firmly enough so the rake doesn't flip over. Feel it? That's the smooth feel of the rake on the sand. And when you . . . There . . . Feel that scraping?"

"Yes. That?"

"Yeah, that's a clam. You feel that? Move over it.

That's it. Pull back. No, not so deep. Just a firm draw
back."

"Yes. I have it."

"Good. Now you turn the handle and it falls into the
basket. Yes. Now lift it to you."

In the wire basket at the rake's end they saw the
four-inch clam, gray and cream.

"Is that a good one?"

"Perfect. If they're smaller than about two or two
and a half inches, throw them back to grow and breed.
If they're bigger than, say, five, they get heavy, they're
better for chowder. So throw those back too. And any
clam that's not closed tight. And be careful of the rake
prongs; they're sharp."

He tossed the clam into the floating potato basket
with the others. He'd done well. He hadn't fooled
around. And she'd stayed still. She hadn't backed her
lovely backside into . . . But that way lay badness. Let
me not think on it. Frailty, thy name is Leonard
Schwartz.

"Shall we have lunch now?" Natasha asked.

She was being as good as gold, as honey. Her eyes
were so large and black. "Why don't we wait? We have
four clams so far. What with the boat rental and the
basket and inner tube—"

"And don't forget that the bandit charged for these
old clam rakes."

"Yeah. With all that, so far nature's free bounty has
run to about thirty-five bucks per clam. Let's have lunch
at two dozen."

"One dozen."

"A compromise—half-past one."

They worked around the sand bar several hundred
yards off Jessup's Neck. Boats passed east toward

Shelter Island and west into Peconic. Small sails appeared in regatta off Robins Island point.

"Len, I have another. It's easy!"

"Great. Put them in your pockets. When they're full I'll come over with the basket."

Within ten minutes he'd come across a large bed and had eighteen clams bobbing in the basket. Natasha added her three.

"Three and a half," she said as they got into the rented aluminum boat. "Half of that first one was mine. Want a salami or ham and cheese?"

They sat in the boat with sandwiches, beer and Schwartz's seltzer, looking across to the beach on the Morton Refuge where a few boat parties were picnicking.

Natasha slipped off her shorts. She was in a bikini bottom. "I suppose if I took off the T-shirt I'd be flirting."

"Thanks for not taking it off. Please."

"Yes. I think I'm being very good. Don't you, Len?"

"Yes. Let's talk about—"

"Look. A cigarette boat. It must be doing seventy! And here's an even better change of a subject—where'd you learn clamming? I thought the East River was polluted?"

"It's almost as unbelievable. When I was a kid my father took me clamming in Jamaica Bay, off Canarsie Beach. I don't suppose Canarsie Beach means anything to you."

"No. It sounds like a place in a Coppola film."

"Brooklyn, yes. And the clams were good. Jesus. I don't think there's any safe clamming now in South Oyster or Great South or even in Moriches Bay. Not until Shinnecock or up here in Peconic. Hey, that cigarette's doing eighty! Maniac!"

They watched the thin blue boat whiz out of sight, a high plume of spray arching from it like the tail feathers of a fighting cock.

"Maybe there'll be a thunderstorm tonight," she said.

"Natasha, what do you think now about Soloff and the mushrooms?"

She looked at him. "A terrible mistake. I can't believe he'd want...Look, how could killing you and Karen have taken the pressure off? You said that this policeman's uncle—Gallagher, was it?—put you onto this. And he's a top cop, right?"

"Right."

"An accident, I really think so. And maybe if you'd had less of it or had been more used to wild mushrooms, the good ones, which made up most of it, you wouldn't have been so badly affected. Vladimir couldn't count on you to gobble it all up like that."

"Right."

She turned her back to him and put her bikini top on under her T-shirt, took off the T-shirt and jumped over the side. "I'm swimming to the beach. You?"

"No. I'll stay with the boat. The tide's coming in and I don't want the boat swinging into the sandbar. We can maybe do an hour's more clamming when you get back, before the water gets too high."

The boat seemed all right. He watched her swim with slow strokes that moved her fast and nearly splashless through the water. Then she turned and swam parallel to the beach. A roar. Schwartz turned. The same cigarette boat cut between him and the beach. It whirred and screeched and cut the water in a skid, curling a ten foot wall of spray off its side.

Stupid bastard. It was way too fast. If anyone had been swimming . . . Jesus! Natasha had been swimming there a few minutes before. Schwartz narrowed his eyes, but the boat was too far down the shore. All he saw was that it held only its driver.

Natasha waved from the beach. He waved back. She motioned toward the low hill jungled with vine behind the beach. He nodded, raised his arm and drew his hand across its middle, hoping it was clear he meant half an hour.

Then he snoozed. He woke. Fifteen minutes. He snoozed. He woke in shade and it was an hour later. He rubbed his eyes. Nothing on the beach. The other picnickers were gone, no moored boats. Natasha wasn't there or in the water, and the boat was pulling on its anchor. He jumped into water halfway up his chest. Well, there was no danger now of the boat running aground, so he could clam for another half an hour or so and get a couple dozen more, by which time Natasha would have returned and they could make it back to the car before the rain.

He moved off with rake and line and floating basket to where he'd found all those clams before lunch. They weren't there or this wasn't exactly the place. Well, he'd follow this line.

None, none, none, and then a lot of sea grass and then he caught himself going too deep; he knew that by the pull on his shoulders. And then the light touch on the handle was gone. He knew that by the wire basketfuls of stones and mud and empty shells he dredged.

He turned at the noise. The damned bright blue cigarette boat again. Idiot. He lifted the seven foot clam rake over his head. The idiot saw him and swerved out a few hundred yards and went up past the sandbar. What the hell was it doing by his boat? The idiot had slowed and was leaning out. What . . . A gaff? What the hell . . .

"Hey!" Schwartz shouted. But it was too far; he'd moved five hundred yards or so down from the mooring. The idiot had lifted the anchor. Oh, Jesus, the idiot was a boat thief. Look at that, and not another boat around! Shit.

The driver leaned from the blue boat to Schwartz's, fastening a line. Schwartz was wading as fast as he could. If the thief would only fall asleep right now for ten or fifteen minutes, he'd get to him. The sleek blue boat drew into the bay, Schwartz's dumpy yet overpriced rental bobbing happily behind.

Overpriced and now stolen, and of course he'd left his MasterCard details with the rental bandit at the Shinnecock Canal. He saw the boats dwindle past Robins Island, headed for the North Fork. And that was the last of them. Terrific. What now?

"Shit!" he shouted, slamming the clam rake down into the water. It came to rest on a large bed of clams. Well, why not? This way it might only come to seventy five clams a clam.

The wind was picking up, but he raked clams. If he worked fast he kept warm, and with a couple dozen more he'd go ashore and find . . .

A small figure was coming out of the dark green hill onto the sand path to the beach. Yes. She stopped, looked around and waved to his waving clam rake. She lifted her hands, palms up. A good question, he thought. Gone for a boat ride. No, she was pointing, waving at someone else. Ah, good, about time Another boat; they'd . . .

What? The fucking thief? What did he want now, the clams? Jesus, coming right at him!

Schwartz waved the rake and waved the rake and fell under water as the boat came on him. A roar of water churned down. He held the rake and pushed to the side and came up gasping to see the boat skid sideways, turning to come at him again, between him and the shore.

Who . . . This was stupid! He knew he had to wait until the boat was close so that he could stay under as it passed. Maybe the clam rake . . .

He held it midway up the wooden shaft for leverage, prongs up. Here the bastard was.

The handle hit into his stomach like a horse's kick, doubling him over, knocking him under, mouth open in a groan. The boat hit the back of his thigh and buttock so hard it straightened him and he went flat on his face down to the bottom. This time he came up retching silt and salt water.

He crouched, holding his stomach and butt. The cigarette boat was turning again. It had to be Whelehan's driver; he was wearing a hood! Whelehan probably bought the things by the half dozen. The beach—if he could only . . . Natasha wasn't there now. Oh, god, had she set him up? No, no . . .

Something bumped. The clam basket bobbed unharmed. He picked out a three incher and another in his other hand. He couldn't go on like this, but he'd have to make it good. Why was the tide rising so fast? Why was that windshield so small?

He threw the clam. It hit. The boat swerved away as he ducked, and he didn't have to go under. But the driver had only been startled by the impact. The bastard would figure that out. The bastard.

He should swim for shore; he saw the boat was farther away. A current in the rising tide pulled him to the side and out.

He began his mediocre crawl. Maybe the current would dump him on a beach before he drowned. Maybe after. He tried to keep his spirits up by imagining his body on the beach—the silent crowd, the coroner, the final cost per clam. He heard the boat roar up behind him.

4

Three, four, he didn't know how many times the boat swiped at him, driving him out deeper, making sure he was well locked into the current. Thunder rolled overhead from gray-black clouds when Schwartz became aware the boat was gone.

And well it might be: it had done its work. He was now in a current far too strong to swim against. He'd been trying to trick it, to sneak diagonally across it toward shore, but now he saw he was held midway between the shore and what must be the tip of Robins Island. And not one boat. He turned onto his back again and floated.

The first time he'd been relaxed and tired enough to do this he thought he'd saved himself. Now he knew he'd merely saved himself to sink a little later. His right side down from the base of his spine was rigid with a

charley horse the size of charley's herd. If he died with
a bad joke in his head, what would happen to his soul?
Nothing. He wasn't a believer. Thank God.

An even worse joke was how he'd finally untied the
rope, watched the clams float off and *then* thought,
"Inner tube!"

Lighting. Good. Hit by lightning would be faster.
But it wasn't so nice to see.

He turned over into his crawl and gave the stroke its
most literal meaning. His arms barely broke water, and
his left hand, when under, kept rubbing what felt like a
small oxyacetylene lance burning where the clam rake
had punched his stomach.

It wasn't Whelehan, of course, behind the wheel.
But where did he get all his heavies? Why should they
do these things for him?

In a crash of thunder Schwartz said, "Ho, ho." He
fell into a dog paddle as useful as any other stroke.
Whelehan got his heavies—drivers for earthmovers,
cigarette boats, fucking F-111's if it came to that—just
where any clever cop on the make could. Once you
were seriously compromised, a whole new sleazy world
opened. And didn't he know it. How different were
they, after all—compromised Ginger and compromised
Schwartz? He couldn't bear to think of that. Just stay
afloat . . .

All of your life was supposed to appear before you,
not just your much wronged wife naked and your son's
balletic spin making the double play at second.

At least he'd left his wallet in the car. They could put
the funeral on MasterCard.

Oh, Karen, Karen. He was so tired. If he could pretend . . .

Schwartz lay his cheek on the water. It felt surpris-

ingly soft and warm. If the thunder would just shut up
and someone would turn off the lightning . . .

He lifted his head from the water into water. The
water in the air was rain. Oh. He'd better float. No, the
hell with it. The light would only keep him awake.

He said, "Good night." The words made him afraid,
but only for a moment. He wanted to pull some water
over him like a comforter, but aside from that and a
vague ache in his belly he felt nothing. He shrugged
into the water and fell asleep.

They were waking him. The bastards. Let him sleep.
Just . . . It was so cold. The shouting bastards.

"Lenny, Jesus, hold on!"

Shaking him from bed. The bed was wet.

"Let me sleep." He opened his eyes. Gallagher.
"What?"

"Never mind. You're okay. This girl saved your life.
She called the city; they called me in Westhampton.
Here's another blanket. You'll be back soon. It's abso-
lutely pissing with rain."

"Why are you out here? I thought . . . What girl?"

Schwartz wriggled onto his elbows in the bottom of
the boat. Who was driving?

Over his shoulder, Whelehan asked, "Are you all
right, Len?"

"Whelehan?"

"Yeah," Gallagher said, his heavy hand tapping
Schwartz's shoulder. "I got hold of Ginger right away. I
knew he was good with boats and knew these waters.
With the girl's . . ."

"Natasha," came her voice.

"Yeah. With her help," Gallagher continued.

Natasha's face appeared out of a yellow slicker. "I

ran out to the road and found a phone. Someone was
trying to drown you."

"Mmm, yes." Schwartz began to shiver; the shivers
woke him. "L-l-lucky for me you found Ginger t-to
help. At home, were you, S-Sergeant?"

"Yes, I was. But, heck, anyone who knows these
waters would figure you'd have been out here with the
current in this tide. I mean, the lady, here—"

"Natasha," she said.

"Yes, she told me where she'd last seen you, so . . ."

"I see," said Schwartz, giving a small ironic handclap in his head to Ginger's "heck," killer as cute puppy
dog.

"Anyway," Ginger went on, "we weren't out fifteen—"

"Hey, Ginger," came Gallagher's loud voice, "do us
a favor and shut up."

And then they were at the Shinnecock Canal.

"Y-yes, I'm all right. Much better now, thanks,
T-Tom," Schwartz said, standing on his own as they
docked.

But stepping on the gunwhale, his right leg gave
way, and he reached out to feel a shoulder supporting
him and then the honey curly hair came up under his
arm so that Natasha helped push him onto the dock
while he clutched her slicker to keep from falling.

And there, bareheaded in the rain, was Karen.

"Karen. Oh, d-darling," he said, faint with the pain
and exhaustion and, now, the joy.

Karen's eyes flicked to his right, and then she looked
at him and said quietly, "You prick. We're through,"
and turned and walked away.

He turned his head. Natasha still supported him. In
the clutching commotion at the dock, her slicker had

unsnapped wide open so that even the most nearsighted of wives, which Karen was not, could see that Natasha was stark naked.

"Oh, sh-shit! Karen, wait! N-Natasha. Oh, shit, Natasha, z-z-zip that. Oh, s-snap it up. Oh, please," he whined, letting go of her so she could.

Schwartz fell down in dockside sand and mud and squeezed his eyes shut like a drowning man or little boy in tantrum.

5

"Tom, this is a decent cup of coffee."

Gallagher stopped his mug halfway to his mouth. "Gee, thanks. And I tie my own shoelaces and can iron shirts too. Ain't that something?"

"I didn't mean—"

"The hell you didn't. You think I've gotten grand and out of touch because I've made this rank. Well, maybe I do have to spend too much time with the paperwork, but I'm still a cop, like you. So what about it? Enough chills gone so you feel up to talking now?"

They faced each other across the white, C-shaped desk in Karen's study—her publisher Bob's hard white book-lined study—where Schwartz had insisted they sit after his hot shower and change because if he came in here where she worked, maybe . . .

"Yes. Let's go," Schwartz said, pulling his blanket tight around his bathrobe.

"Well, let's start with your little clam digging adventure."

"Okay. Last night I invited Natasha to go clamming. I wanted to test her loyalties. This was in the presence of her grandparents, the old Kalubins. And then I did some very simple, old-fashioned snooping, following Natasha back to her parents' house. I heard her tell Helen, her mother, about it. I knew she would; they're very close."

Schwartz stopped to watch Gallagher pour some of the Jameson he'd set out into his coffee. It was Bob's whiskey—another item to replace. How could he replace Karen? "Yes, so Natasha told Helen and then Helen told Alexei, Natasha's father, or anyhow they talked. I couldn't hear the words. But then Alexei came back into the kitchen for some water, and I heard him call Soloff and tell him, and Soloff obviously told Whelehan of our proposed outing. It wasn't hard for Whelehan to figure where we'd rent the boat and the general area we'd be in."

"Yeah. The rental place got a call asking if you'd gone out from there."

"And of course they had my name from the credit card deposit."

"We're checking on that boat and driver, from the description you and the girl—"

"Natasha. Come on, Tom. It's not so hard to say. Na-ta-sha. Natasha."

"Yeah, Natasha," he repeated, so that its "tash" rhymed with "trash." "But there's not gonna be a trace. Ginger gets good bad guys to work for him."

"Ah, at last you've come round to thinking the nephew somewhat at fault."

"Sure. And that guy driving the bulldozer? A big bad record—graduated Attica twice. Mostly he worked Westchester, but we pulled some stuff he did here in Suffolk County. B and E and larceny and found that my nephew was involved. Listen, Lenny, I ah, owe you an... I, ah. At the start of all this I did sort of tell Ginger he'd better watch himself. You know, the proper family thing to do. You know. But I swear to God from when you got poisoned I didn't give that jerk the time of day. I know Ginger's a bad cop. I'm interested in finding out how bad."

"By what, by letting him kill me?"

"I can't *make* you go on, Lenny, but, Jesus, you know he doesn't want to kill you."

Across the room from Schwartz was the house's only non-modern piece of art—a long Chinese painting from the early nineteenth century. Two golden carp swam through watercolor water of gray brown clouds. The lower fish had its two bulged eyes turned up. The top fish had its mouth half open and its upper lip curled back in a playful sneer. It was funny and very serene.

"It's not that simple," Schwartz said. "It came to me out in the water that Ginger is very ambivalent and that while he's still superficially okay, the hinges are working off his mind pretty quickly. I mean, scaring me so that I *might* have drowned seems like he wanted it both ways. Unless it was the driver who fouled up. But I don't think so. It would have been tough to prove as premeditated murder, even with witnesses. But it was no sure thing, and he should have known it wouldn't scare me. You see, he knows me. He's studied me, maybe even seen my records. Not from you, I know that. He's very unpredictable. He has me confused."

"Look, Lenny," Tom said, and tipped back the coffee and sat the empty mug on the desk. "I know you're going through a bad time personally. You and Karen. Well, once we could . . . You and I would have talked about it and . . . But we're not so close now and I suppose that's that." He looked across at Schwartz.

"That's that."

"Yeah, well, anyway, I want you to know I understand. I mean, I know that something else is at stake here for you. So . . ."

"So isn't that a dandy piece of luck for you—how I'm so personally locked into this."

"I was going to say—so maybe we should stop it here. Sure, there's more of this mess to reveal, but, shit, there's enough on Ginger for at least a discharge, if not a sentence."

Schwartz sipped the cooling coffee and looked past Gallagher. That offer had been no offer at all, and Gallagher knew it. He took a big swallow and the top carp leered from the painting on the wall. He said, "But that leaves Soloff. And the land deed. And Amboys. It pretty much leaves everything, including whatever state level favor you're doing. The only good thing so far is that they've been forced to release John Johnson."

"Who? Oh, yeah, the half-wit Indian. Yeah, that's something. But, as you say, there's much bigger business about the land."

"The land, the land. Tom, what is it that Albany knows and you know and I don't know?"

"Nothing. I'm getting more coffee. You should drink more hot stuff," said Gallagher, heaving up and taking both mugs, "even if it doesn't have good Irish whiskey in it."

"It also doesn't have Lethe water," Schwartz said as Tom returned.

"Whatsat?"

"That's Albany and you. Tom, I know why I'm sticking in here with this mess—to nail a really crooked, arrogant cop and a whole police force closing ranks around him. And spare me the wise nod which means you think it's my guilt. You've got no right . . . Anyway, now, as you know, there's more to it. It's about me and Karen and my stupid fooling around and this awful Rasputin Karen takes to be Rembrandt. So I have to see it all through. But what's the deal for you? Some politician in Albany trying to get someone down here who's involved with the land deal through Soloff or Troost?"

Gallagher nodded at the Jameson. "Can I have another? . . . Thanks. No, there's nothing tricky like that. And I'm not wasting our time saying more." He sniffed the steam off the top of the coffee and took a delicate sip. "Hey, all the paintings and stuff here—you like it?"

"I wouldn't choose to live with it, for the most part. But this old one—what do you think?"

Gallagher half turned and cocked his head at the wall behind him. "Yeah. It's okay. Better than the others. But who needs to look at popeyed goldfish? I'm a red snapper or bluefish man myself, especially if they're on a plate, ha!"

Schwartz thought to say "You art what you eat," but thought better of it. He said, "Okay. All I want from you is some surveillance on Whelehan light enough so that it doesn't keep him from the action. I have this theory."

Gallagher drummed on the desk with his fingers. "I

can give you light surveillance. I guess by now you've figured I really can't give you much more, like assigning some of our men out here. One or two state people on surveillance and that's it. Oh, and me, of course. I'll be there if it gets rough. So what's this theory? Am I going to like it?"

"I think Whelehan and Soloff are into a crazy sort of competition. Given what I know of Ginger, I wonder that they can work together at all. Let's say a problem comes up and it's Whelehan's department to solve it. But he's not completely successful and Soloff is contemptuous. Arrogant. Well, this makes Whelehan try something wilder the next time. It doesn't quite work and Soloff remains unimpressed. So then Whelehan—"

"Wait, Jesus, wait! Lenny, you saying all this is going on and they don't know about it, not consciously?"

"Yes."

"I thought you were. You're still exhausted and in shock, so I'll be nice. Otherwise I'd tell you I think your theory's full of shit."

"Why?"

Gallagher held the bottle, looking at the label. He began rolling the bottle back and forth in his hand. "I said I wouldn't discuss it now 'cause you're in bad shape. But supposing you were right. How would this help nail Ginger or Soloff?"

"I don't know."

"You don't know. That's the first sensible part of your theory. You better get some sleep now, and I have to get back to town early tomorrow."

As they walked through the living room, Gallagher said, "Like that, that one. What would that go for, about?"

"I'm not up on prices, Tom. I don't know. Maybe two fifty, three fifty, four."

"You're really . . . You really saying hundreds of thousands? Jesus, there's gotta be ten suckers born every minute and they've gotta be stinking rich."

"Oh, I don't know—de Kooning's local. Maybe they like that."

"Don't pull my leg," Gallagher said by the door.

"Don't pull mine either, Tom. Don't screw around with me, or yourself, for some state legislature creep in Albany who may or may not remember this favor you're doing."

"I don't know what you're talking about, you wise bastard. Get some sleep and try to stay dry. I can't keep pulling you out."

After he'd closed the door Schwartz thought how Gallagher kept throwing him in. No, damn it. Gallagher didn't have to; he threw himself in. Whelehan a rival of Soloff? What about Schwartz and Soloff? Schwartz and Gallagher? Schwartz and Whelehan and Schwartz. He put himself to bed sounding like a list of law firms.

6

He woke fighting the old paranoia: everyone couldn't be guilty. Troost, for example, who was guilty, had confessed and so wasn't, in that way, guilty. He mustn't let himself become suspicious of Troost's confession, the single ray of sunshine that emphasized the clouds.

It was a clear bright morning after the storm. He'd run and shower. If they were watching, good; they'd watch him run.

He stepped out of the shower, put the towel around him and answered the repaired telephone.

"Inspector Schwartz?"

"Yes?"

"This is Harold Beck, Chief of Southampton Police."

"Yes. Good morning, Chief Beck. How are you?"

"Fine, sir. I wanted to formally apologize for any-thing you feel has been a lack of cooperation on our part. It won't continue. Detective Sergeant Whelehan has been put on suspension pending our investigation of certain matters."

"That's good news. I appreciate that."

"I'm glad. I hope that means you'll let us handle everything from here on."

"Oh, yes. Go on and handle whatever you want, Chief."

"What I'm getting at, Inspector, is that I hope you'll now withdraw your own informal and, I have to say, irregular investigation."

"Ah. Why?"

"In the first place, you'll appreciate that the presence of a high-ranking officer from outside this force looking into our affairs with no formal charges or investigative brief is very damaging to morale. And as a result, we've had to suspend the finest young officer we've seen around here for . . . Well, let that go. But another thing is the scrapes you seem to get into. We get huge bills from a leading local shop, houses smashed, old people in the hospital in shock, missing boats. Look, just keeping up with this is costing our taxpayers a great deal of money."

"I am sorry about my effect on morale, but I can live with that and so can your force. And my scrapes are someone else's idea to rough me up, maybe even with a nod and wink from your direction. You would have saved your taxpayers money by putting the finest young officer Whelehan away before this started. And from what I know, that should have been years ago."

"I hear you, Inspector. The other thing I called about was to tell you that as part of *my* investigation, I'm filing a report on what I consider to be your gross misconduct with the New York City First Deputy Commissioner and with the Deputy Commissioner of Legal Matters."

"Good. Two very thorough and responsible people. Thanks for your call, Chief. I think you're doing exactly the right thing."

"Just lay off, Inspector Schwartz. This may be the way they do things in your sewer of a city, but it's not how we operate out here."

"Now, Chief. We're all professionals. Calm down and have a nice—"

"I think you're a filthy—"

"Chief! Before you say it: you do know my phone's being tapped?"

In the loud click Schwartz smiled. Yes, he was going to have a nice day. The run had been good; this call was better, and after cereal and coffee, it would get best. If, as Gallagher said, he couldn't have the cowboys, he'd better powwow with the Indians.

7

Detective Inspector Leonard Schwartz sat with Chief Sun Johnson and two tribal elders in the tin roof shade of a veranda. They drank lemonade and sat on rocking chairs and talked. Schwartz talked twice as much as the Chief; the elders just listened. At the end of two hours Sun Johnson put up his hand and turned to the elders. One put up his hand. The other thought, nodded and put up his. They stood and shook hands all around.

Then Schwartz and the Chief went on a shopping party into Southampton. First they went to Brown's 10¢—25¢—$1 & UP store taking no chances. By squeezing, they made the four large sacks fit into the trunk. Then they went to Lillywhites Sporting Goods. When the bill was totaled Schwartz bit the bullet and handed over his credit card.

And after they'd unloaded at the reservation, the Chief asked Schwartz to wait. He came back with his big, shambling grandson.

"Thank you, sir," John said, slowly, mechanically, at his grandfather's prod.

It was awkward. Schwartz put out his hand.

John took it, squeezed and said, "It was very bad. They were bad to me. I didn't do that, what they said."

He smiled then, and a tear came out of his eye onto the side of his nose.

Schwartz patted his shoulder and left.

Two o'clock. A very good and efficient day, so far. If he didn't think of Karen, this was going to be an excellent day.

Cowboys and Indians. He decided to call Natasha before she called him, to head her off at her pass, as it were.

As it was, Helen told him Natasha had been invited to Baldock Island and should be there now. Would he call her? Was there any message? And how was he, really?

No, no and really fine.

Natasha was on Baldock with Karen, who he wouldn't think of. And with Soloff. Cozy and cozier, And that wasn't counting Whelehan. Whelehan was unaccountable.

He dialed Baldock Island. The phone was answered by a butler impersonating Mowbray or Treacher's impersonation of a butler. Schwartz resisted asking for Bertie Wooster. He asked for John Unicorn Baldock. And he should say it was the police calling.

"Unicorn Baldock here," slouched a voice from the phone.

"This is Inspector Schwartz, sir. I'd like—"

"Inspector? Oh, ha. I thought it was really the police, not . . . Oh, well, I mean I feel we're, though we haven't actually met, friends and from what I hear of you you're, ha, a far cry from the ordinary . . . Well, ha, ha," said Baldock slackly, louchely.

"Mr. Baldock—"

"Unicorn, please."

"Uni . . ." Schwartz couldn't. "I assure you, sir, I'm

a police officer. A cop, a flatfoot, though a flatfoot of some rank."

"A rank flatfoot?"

"Not bad, Mr. Bal . . ."

"Oh, see here, if you can't handle the whole Unicorn, call me John or Corny, though there are naughtier nicknames too."

"I'd like to come out there tomorrow, as a police officer, to talk with Vladimir Soloff. Will he be there?"

"Oh, this is marvelous—*so* official! Yes, Len . . . May I call you Len?"

"Yes, yes. Will he—"

"He'll be here. And your wonderful Karen, of course. And Natasha, whom I believe you *know*, and a few close friends who don't count. And the too wonderful Madame."

"Madame?"

"My dear boy. None other—but you mustn't breathe to anyone, this island is her very special retreat."

"Who?"

"Miss Perdita Lawless!"

"Who?"

"What? I am surprised. I thought you a man of—"

"The old actress? I didn't know she was still alive."

"She is very much alive and very beautiful! Oh, you have no idea. Come. You'll see. She is La Suprema! Well, shall we send a boat?"

"Yes. Ten in the morning?"

"Yes, ten. At the town dock in Sag Harbor. You'll recognize the boat: it flies the Baldock coat of arms."

"Right, and I'll be the half-drowned one on the pier."

"Oh? Oh, yes! You've had such adventures! Len, should I inform Karen?"

"Yes. Please. You tell everyone that I'll be on the island tomorrow."

He felt he didn't have to mention Whelehan. If Whelehan didn't already know his plans, he'd know later, in plenty of time. And now he could relax and not think of Karen.

~~~~~~ 8

It was an old Chris-Craft speedboat in two-tone mahogany, which reminded Schwartz of certain station wagons of the fifties and of that convertible, the, the . . .

"Chrysler Town and Country," said Jack the boatman. He also said that he did like working for Mr. Baldock because it sure beat ten years as a bayman and freezing his keister and breaking his back for nothing: he and his wife and the girl had to live with his parents, but now they'd bought a house at North Haven. And, sure, Mr. B. was a character, but wasn't everyone, when you thought about it?

"How many others work out there?" Schwartz asked.

"Let's see. Wolf, the butler—"

"Wolf?"

"Yes. He's English or something, I think. Wolf and old Sissy, and cook and Jeremy indoors. Jeremy also drives. Then me and Freddy Phillips on boats. And Walter, the gardener, and he has one, two, four others.

They also work on the shore and erosion, you know. Um, then there's Sandor. Mr. B. says 'Shandor.' He's the gamekeeper and he has two assistants for the pheasant and deer and other stuff. And that's it."

Schwartz considered: a staff of fourteen, so if push came to shove he'd be pushed and shoved. "Many guests there now?"

"Besides your wife, Ms. Walker, there's Mr. Soloff and Miss Lawless and Miss Kalu . . . Kalubik, I think. And then three gentlemen from, I heard, New Orleans. I don't know the names."

"No one named Whelehan? A local policeman?"

"No, nobody else."

The boat came around Cedar Point into the open waters of Baldock Bay.

"Is that the island out there? It looks big."

"Yes, that's it. It's about five or six miles long and three at its widest, where you see the hill."

Under the wind made by the boat, Schwartz felt the heat. It hit the water in thick shimmers and waved the air over the bay. As they approached, the island looked less miragelike; it grew bigger, tailed off south and deepened at its northern end in wooded hills. They headed for an area of low dunes and salt marsh. And then there was a narrow dock: a few posts, a few planks and lots of gaps.

"The main docks are up the other end, but Mr. B. likes to meet new visitors here, sort of to give them the tour. He should be right along," Jack said, handing Schwartz his satchel. "See you."

"Thanks." The dock went into a shallow beach, eight or so feet deep at this tide. It was a coarse light sand streaked with gray mud and littered with clamshells and bits of blue point and the dun-colored shields of horseshoe crabs. The dunes behind were held in a mesh of wild cranberry, out of which grew low bush bayberry and heavier beach plum, some of whose small fruit had started ripening so that a dusty rose spread upward on the green. On top of the dune, Schwartz looked across hundreds of acres of salt marsh. Two great blue herons rose flapping and dangle-footed toward the wooded hills. A few hundred yards beyond, a deer lifted its head from shoulder high sea grass.

If Baldock thought this would impress visitors, he was right. Here was the track; Schwartz heard an engine now. A strange vehicle came toward him: a triple length jeep, open, with a sort of roll bar between the front and back seats, and that must be Baldock standing, holding on to it, waving, in orange, an orange jumpsuit, a white hat with a long visor, a white scarf, a smile, smiling, leaning down to shake his hand like the Viceroy of India in an old motorcade or new return-to-the-Raj flick.

"Hello, Len. Marvelous you're here. You're so good-looking! If you don't mind . . . Karen couldn't . . . Vladimir's doing her. Her portrait, I mean. But here's Natasha. Natasha? So quiet? And look how we've fixed her up in one of our *fait-tout* jumpies and I think she's rather dreamy in it, don't you? And that's it; jump in back here. There's plenty of room in our old JP—jeep phaeton. Stand, you'll see more. Hold on here. All right, Jeremy, let's loop around the Deep Pond end and then up Royal Bay side, shall we, and then I can tell you the history, Len," said John Unicorn Baldock, taking his first breath.

He was a handsome man if you didn't look close. If, like Schwartz, you did, the makeup and hair dye and face-lifts moved so that you worried if the wind wouldn't blow it all down, leaving you to grip the rail

beside Roderick Usher or Dorian Gray, all of which was
nearly curious enough to keep you from looking down
at Natasha in her white semi-see-through jumpsuit so
unzipped that . . .

"What history?"

Baldock leaned close. "The story. You may have
heard two, the first of which I'm prepared to verify.
Yes, I am the direct descendant of Sir John Unicorn
Royston-Baldock, to whom King Charles the Second of
Blessed Memory gave the manor of the island in perpe-
tuity in 1663. But as to the second, I say nothing, one
way or the other. Oh, that's the herd of fallow deer we
keep and that's Deep Pond. Excellent mussels and we do
our own oysters there, where you see the sticks. That
other story is about how no Baldock for seven genera-
tions now has had any discernable employment, and that
the fortune we live on—interest off interest off interest,
à la some Boston people I really could name—is based
on finding Captain Kidd's treasure on the island all
those years back, in the eighteenth century. Well, to all
that I say absolutely *rien de tout*! Oh, and you see that
green hat with the feather and tufts? There, there. It's on
the head of Sandor Ormay, our genuine Hungarian master of the game. Not that there's much shooting nowa-
days, though there are still some who like to get out the
old Purdy and bang away, like our friend Vladimir—
I'm an over and under man, myself. But, no, it's mostly
the ecological work these days, although the deers need
culling. Well, rabbits are nothing to those deers, my
dear. So we cull. Some we ship off to the upstate game
reserves. We have fallow and some whitetail and red,
and we're starting—not to shoot but to see if we can
help an endangered species—a breeding program with

those tiny key deer, you know, from down Key West.
Well, not exactly Key West which would be far too sophisticated for those simple creatures, but my good
friend David, who knows everything, arranged to ship
me two and we are hoping shortly, Sandor and I, to
announce an accouchement," he said, and took his second breath.

"How's Karen?" Schwartz asked Natasha, to add to
the confusion. He saw her sigh and try to smile and felt
bad for her and felt how in another life they might . . .
But no.

"She's so angry, and I didn't mean to hurt her that
way. And if I knew what I know now . . . I wouldn't
have, but . . . Len . . . " she shouted up.

Baldock, touching Natasha's and then Schwartz's
shoulder, said, "Oh, my dears. What a situation! Ne'er
mind. All will be well in the healing air of this en-
chanted isle."

If this was Prospero, Schwartz wondered, what
would Caliban be like?

"All I want now is to be able to apologize to Karen,"
Natasha shouted, "to have her be able to hear me."

Now they drove up the eastern side of the island.
Suddenly, Baldock sat down, shut his eyes and slept,
but whether from boredom, madness or the metabolic
dive off speed or cocaine, Schwartz couldn't tell.

The track curved inland around a large pond, its
center flocked with geese and ringed with snowy egret
and white heron. And then it rose into a wood of immense oak and elm and straight maple and the odd
white line of silver birch.

Schwartz sat back beside Natasha. On her other side,
Baldock seemed to be snoring.

"Natasha, I hope not, but things might get nasty," Schwartz said through his cupped hand into her ear. "You'd be best staying out of it. But if you have to be involved, you'd better be on my side."

She cupped her hand to his ear: "Yes, but you'd better be fair to Vladimir. Don't goad him so that you can legally murder him. Yes?"

He nodded. Karen must have said something... Karen said something to Soloff who... Oh, damn it, damn it.

Damn! Look at that, he said to himself as the Manor House appeared on its hill. He'd seen bigger and older, but never in this country so big and old a house. It had a two story, gabled center wing of rough stone, with a wooden cupola, and flanking this were two large wings of white wood. He saw from the line of brick chimneys how wings went back and connected so that the overall house shape was square, probably around a central courtyard. From behind the architecture came the sound of shooting.

The jeep drew up near the front stone stairs. Jeremy honked the horn. A tall blond beast of a butler loped down, told Schwartz in his Hollywood manservant voice that he was Wolf, which Schwartz believed, and he whistled. Would it bring two- or four-footed response?

It brought four in the shapes of a very stout woman who rocked her way down the steps beside a man who yelled to Schwartz that he was the underbutler. And though Jack the boatman hadn't mentioned this position, who was Schwartz to gainsay him? He was about six four, muscle-bound, in tight white T-shirt on which was printed a map of Baldock Island, and his black hair was one inch wide and one half inch high and began over his nose and ran over the middle of his shaven skull and seemingly never stopped, or went anyhow down the Mohawk trail into the back of the T-shirt. He wore a small steel ring through his left nostril. Well, why not a punk underbutler? And Jeremy got out so that the four servants, two at arms and two at the legs, carried the snoring John Unicorn Baldock into his Manor House, his mannered house. Why not?

Schwartz, still in the jeep, put his chin in his hands and began counting the reasons why not. He was also, he understood, waiting for the next scene in the Masque of the Anarchic Rentier. Natasha, going up the stairs, said that when he came in someone would show him to his room. She said she should tell him that it would be his own room, not Karen's.

Why not? He sat in the jeep. The shooting had stopped, and so here was the cue for . . .

"Hello, Vladimir. Did you get my message?"

"Hi, Len. Of course. At your disposal entirely," he said, shifting the open shotgun across his left forearm to shake hands. He saw Schwartz's glance. "Rather nice, isn't it?"

"Very Purdy."

"Holland and Holland, actually. You know guns well?"

"Hardly at all. I don't even know much about the one I carry."

"Well, I cannot tell you how good it is to see you here so that we can finally clear up all this—confusion. Please, allow me to show you to your room."

Why not allow Vladimir to show him? After all, he, too, wanted the confusion cleared up. Maybe. He wished he knew where Ginger was. He wouldn't waste his breath asking Soloff. "You were shooting—I thought you were at work on a portrait of Karen."

"No. Whatever gave you that idea?" asked Soloff, lightly, politely opening the door.

~~~~~~~ 9

Lunch would be alfresco. Fine, but the room they'd put him in was diminuendo, chosen for its lack of being near any action, like the inner courtyard with its south-west studio section.

The house was larger and less regular than it had looked from its front. It had, for instance, three floors, not two, in this section where he was—a third floor gable room, very pretty in its subdued, secluded way.

Schwartz set his hairbrush on the maple dresser. Where to hide the gun? Ah, yes. He lay the gun in its holster on the dresser next to the hairbrush; he couldn't play fairer than that. And he left the bedroom door wide open as he went down to find the back terrace and lunch and, who knew, perhaps even his wife.

Karen kissed his cheek and said hello and urged him to the mussel salad vinaigrette, so, why not, he smiled and kissed her cheek hello back and held his plate with its worn coat of Baldock arms, little creatures alternately rampant and couchant, for Claude the chef to fill with mussels and shallots and spinach and cherry tomatoes all under a white dicing of garlic and green patina of dill. They moved down the twenty-foot linened length to where in ice the bottles of champagne stuck out from a large silver tub. Karen found club soda; he took a beer, a Beck's. Beck, like the chief of police, why not. How lovely all this was. How nervous.

Five small tables were set about the terrace. No, the tables were ordinary size; it was the two-hundred-foot-long terrace that diminished them. Below the terrace was a large swimming pool, and below that were formal gardens and then a salt meadow and dunes and the ocean opening beyond. His father was the small ghost leading a phantom picket line along the beach.

"Anywhere we like. John won't be down for lunch, and Vladimir's having his in the studio, and Madame L. never appears until dusk."

At least Karen also couldn't bring herself to call him Unicorn. At a near table three young men in identical black leather shorts and Bundeswehr singlets nodded to them. "Here, let's sit by ourselves," he said.

"Offended by the company?"

"Yes, although the gay hedonist far right doesn't repulse me any more than the straight hedonist far right. Or don't you think?"

"Yes. Sorry."

"Okay, sorry I snapped back. Karen, tell me the ground rules. For instance, if Natasha should turn up to sit with us, would you leave? Should I?"

"Stop projecting. I can cope with Natasha as long as I understand that you're not . . . You may not believe this, but it's been Vladimir who's been explaining the clamming misadventure to me."

"Oh, well, then that makes it fine. Because, as we

know, he's a swell sensible guy who only has our inter-
ests as a devoted couple at heart. Wonderful."

"Maybe it's more like that than—"

"Karen, Karen." He sipped the foam from the top of
his glass and remembered he couldn't take alcohol.
"Have you slept with him?"

"No. Of course not."

He felt the tears come. "I believe you. Oh, shit, I'm
doing it again." He wiped his eyes with the linen napkin. "Karen, be careful. Please. Ginger Whelehan may
be around. He's not just a social climber; he'd do anything to reach the top—including dynamiting the whole
mountain. If there's any sign of trouble, get to your
room, lock the door and get under the bed. Don't,
please don't mistrust me on this." He took her hand.
Was that a returning squeeze? Why not think of it like
that. He stood.

"What are you doing?"

"I'm leaving this delicious lunch that I somehow
can't stomach and I'm going to talk with Soloff in his
studio."

"Be careful—I mean, of Whelehan. Or anything."

"Yes. Oh, yes. Thanks. You too."

Upstairs, he looked into his room. Very nice, very
neat, the hairbrush where he'd left it, the holster where
he'd left it, except empty now. He patted the gun up
under his arm. Someone, he hoped not himself, was
being very dumb.

When he opened the studio door he saw Soloff's
back. Then he saw that he was eating, sitting down.
Then he saw that he was eating, sitting down studying a
portrait of Karen.

"Come in, Len," Soloff said without turning.

Schwartz looked from the threshold. Oh, fuck him.

Oh, the painting was so good and the jealousy came into
his mouth, filled it with bitterness. "If you were a worse
painter, Vladimir, this would be easier."

Soloff turned, smiling. "That, from you, is a compli-
ment."

"It's very . . . it's a very good, very serious painting."

"Thank you. I'm looking at this bit of blue in the
blouse."

The portrait showed Karen seated at a desk, books
open, leaning on a forearm, some worry working the
features of her face. It was beautiful and unflattering.
Schwartz wanted to know everything about it rather than
just stick in the doorway with his bitterness and . . . The
hell with it. To work. He went in.

"I'm the dumb one, Ginger, right?" he said, feeling
the barrel cold on the side of his cheek. He heard the
door close. It was a heavy door.

"You don't know how dumb, Schwartz. Don't turn.
Put your hands up higher. Now keep them right up and
get onto your knees. Now put your right hand in your
pocket. Yes, and I'll just reach in here and take your
other gun. Okay, now get up and sit in that chair over
there by the table. You wouldn't have any more
weapons, would you?"

"No, just the two guns you have. Oh, and the cavalry
is coming and these sneakers have retractable jet en-
gines that—"

The slap spun his head back; the chair banged the
table. Tubes of oil paint jigged up, rolled. Schwartz
heard a few fall off. His eyes were teary.

"I've had all the shit from you I'm going to take,"
Ginger said, standing over him. "I warned you, we both
warned you. But no. Jesus, my uncle must have you by
the short hairs. You could have been smart here, gotten

into some real money. But not you. Well, it's over.
There's too much riding on this. It's my chance to crawl
out of the slime and no one's going to stop me. My
bitch of a wife couldn't and neither will my supercop
shit of an uncle and especially no jewtown wise-ass like
you."

Schwartz knew he had to start on Soloff. Soloff was
nothing, but Soloff was all he had. He didn't want to
start because of what Ginger might do. He wouldn't
think of it. "Vladimir, this ex-cop is nuts. But you don't
have to go down with him. You have better things to
do." Through the blur of tears he saw the disagreeing
shake of Soloff's head.

"I've told Vladimir about the sort of divide-and-con-
quer approach you'd take. Remember, I'm a cop too.
It's no use. You're finished, Schwartz. Put your arms
behind the back of the chair."

He had to make his move now. Schwartz fell forward
toward Whelehan's feet. His face went black. The middle of his face exploded.

"We were going to avoid this, you said."

That was Soloff he heard. Where was he? Oh, Jesus,
his mouth was full of—

"Get up."

Whelehan's voice.

"Get the fuck up. If you try anything else, I'll blow
your fucking head away."

Hadn't he? Schwartz's mouth was full. On his hands
and knees he spat. The soft click sound on the floor was
his tooth. Kicked in the mouth, that was it.

Soloff said, "Do what he says. He really means what
he says."

"You'd better fucking believe it."

He pulled himself onto the chair. It was too bright here. He shut his eyes.

"Here," said Soloff, putting a rag into his hands.

Schwartz put it to his mouth. "Oh. Oush! Fuck, thish hurtsh!" He spat. He held up his hand. "Whelehan. I'm sitting quietly. Let me, please, as one cop to another. Don't do this. Even if I'm not your uncle's best pal, you know I work for him. This is his idea and you know what a proud man he is." He put the rag to his mouth. Good. Whelehan was listening. "He doesn't like you, Ginger. I don't know why. Personally, I think you're a terrific guy as well as a great dropkicker." Schwartz squinted open an eye, half expecting another blow.

Whelehan straddled a chair facing him. His gun pointed between Schwartz's eyes. "Hurry up," he called. Then he said, "Maybe you'd be interested to know that my uncle doesn't worry me, not at all."

Schwartz began to consider this, but then Soloff came over and caught his attention with coils of rope, coils of wire and a plastic clothesline.

"This," said Whelehan, taking the rope. "The plastic stretches and the wire would kill him too fast and leave marks."

"Is this absolutely—" Soloff began.

Ginger cut him short: "Yes."

Schwartz looked up at Soloff, but it was impossible to tell if he was really disturbed or was working some hard-soft partnership under Ginger's tutelage.

Whelehan said, "Schwartz, I'm going to tie you up. You're no match for me. If you think you are, I'll kill you before I tie you up. Makes no difference to me."

Schwartz knew it did—that business about rope rather than wire. But the big pain in his mouth decided to let Ginger get away with fibbing. And, Jesus, every-

one had better show up on time. Or had Ginger fixed
that with his local tamed police force?

Ginger tied him up. There were no flies on Ginger as
a tier-up. When Schwartz tried to expand a forearm
muscle, Ginger's fingers dug right in and made it relax,
and the rope went tighter around. Schwartz managed the
trick a little on his runner's legs, but not, he knew, so it
would make a difference. A strangely demure lament
ran through his head. Oh, dear, he thought. Oh, dear.
Before the blindfold went on, Whelehan gagged him.
Oh, he was so good at this—Inquisition, SS good. Oh,
dear. His last sight of the studio was Karen's beautifully
serious face in oil paint. Maybe Karen was around
watching? She'd follow, save him? Of course not. He
hoped not. Whelehan would—

"We're going to carry you, Schwartz. The blindfold
and gag will make it easier, so don't struggle if you
don't want to hurt yourself."

What the hell was happening? Was he over Whelehan's shoulder? Soloff's? What were those sounds?
Your other senses were supposed to be heightened when
you were deprived of one. Compensation. Bullshit—
now he couldn't feel or hear right. A door. Yes. A few
steps across a floor and stop. Another door and steps?
Steps down, a flight of steps. Another door. Another
flight down?

He'd have to keep swallowing. Lots of little swallows, because if he let the blood build up, he'd choke
on this gag. Stupid to choke when they were going to so
much trouble. . . . An echo of footsteps? Another door.
Cooler. A cellar? Shit! His foot bumped, bent his knee,
hurt it against—

They were putting him down. What? Ouch, shit.

Swallows, small swallows. He was lying half out, half in what? A metal edge across his shoulders and under his thighs. Wheels, he heard the wheels, a wheel, the echo, their footsteps. Cool, definitely. It had to be a wheelbarrow. Some tunnel or passage. So . . . Ouch! So it had been a door in the studio into another room and another door with steps to the cellar. He swallowed. Was there less blood? If he kept swallowing, could he bleed to death? Bleed to death without loss of blood? Was this an old tunnel? A hiding place against Indians or later against the British in the Revolutionary War? Never that. If any place had been pure Tory this was it. Oh, great, another loose tooth. But nothing the morticians couldn't fix.

"Wait." Soloff's voice.

Something turning, squeaking open. Fresh air.

"Have a look." Ginger's voice.

Silence. Sea gulls. "All right." Soloff.

Carried again. Definitely Ginger. What the hell had he meant by saying his uncle didn't worry him at all? Oh, shit, if it meant that Gallagher was somehow in with them, he was really dead. Dead. That bastard. He'd fucking kill Gallagher for killing him. He would have smiled but for the pain in his mouth and lips.

Now outside, the walking on grass or sand. Some sunlight. Now it was all sunlight he felt and thought he saw, too, through the blindfold. Ouch.

They'd dropped him on the ground. Untying him? Yes. What?

"We're untying you and taking off the blindfold. You can walk from here," Ginger said. "Not bad; in a few minutes there won't be any rope marks. No marks except your mouth. But that'll be no big deal, by the time you're found."

Schwartz blinked against the sunlight. They must be on the north, yes, the north shore below the woods. Ginger's gun prodded his spine. He walked. Soloff went in front on a path that followed the line of high reeds edging a marsh.

"Here," Soloff said, stepping off and parting the reeds. "Follow me, please."

Schwartz liked that "please." He was a sucker for politeness. The only way he'd consent to being murdered was with a "please." He'd probably come back to haunt his killers to say "thank yoooo." His legs didn't feel too bad. Was that the great Whelehan tying technique or the slight expansion he'd managed? They were pushing through thick, ten foot high reeds and grass. A narrow path appeared, twisting off toward the shore. What? A shack?

"Stop," said Whelehan. "Turn around. You're going to die in there. But at least you won't die lonely. There'll be plenty of company. This is an eel pen. You like eels?"

"Enough of that, Ginger," Soloff said.

"Well, Schwartzie, any last jewtown joke?"

Schwartz nodded and spat a mouthful of blood over Ginger's face.

Ginger put his pistol to Schwartz's mouth and raised his left hand.

Soloff shouted, "Stop it. It's enough to, to . . . Just don't torture him. Let's get on with it."

Ginger paused, his hand in midair. Then he dropped it, drew the gun back and said, "Get in there."

As Schwartz turned to walk, the punch came into his

kidney. He thought he might be peeing blood and tried not to look down. He looked around. Where was the cavalry? What did Ginger know about Gallagher? Did Karen still love him? He shrugged and got in there.

10

The tide also rises. Clever Ginger. Schwartz was chewing the gag so that he'd have a scream or two before he drowned. A dab hand at tying-up was Ginger. Damned Gallagher, how could he have let this happen? Where was everyone? Anyone?

The shack was long and low. Two glassless window frames let in light from across him on the water side. His mouth hurt. Soloff might not have had Whelehan's superb enthusiasm for the work, but Soloff hadn't hindered, such was his dedication to his own bad cause. There were four eel pens in the shack. He was tied into one, suspended along the length of the gangplank at his side. What was it Fran Jansen had said? Yes—like a trussed duck. Would eels like trussed duck? Eels would eat anything, but of course eels were just Ginger's little joke. Only him and the water here.

The water was at his cheek now. He chewed the gag. There hadn't been eels here for years, nor people. This way . . . What? Well, Ginger might untie him after high tide, let him float out in a week, a month, a year after the next high tide. He couldn't quite figure it, but you had to trust Ginger in these matters. That was one absolutely insane cop. And why, why, why wasn't Ginger worried about his big-shot cop uncle? Fucking Whelehan. Fucking Gallagher. Fucking tide. His neck was stiff from keeping his head up. The shack was built for this run of fresh sea water off the tides.

He tried to spit. Blood dribbled into his mouth. Ginger's face had been splattered, splotched, blotched, blobbed with gobs of . . . No good. The words didn't cheer him. What could he do? If this was a summer vacation, could work be worse?

That didn't do anything, either.

He tried kicking against the rope. Nope. Hopeless. Would he not, even in this hour or less of his death, be serious? Assess his life? He would not. Ginger would knot. His neck muscles would not anymore and his right cheek was in the water, right eye shut.

There, he'd caught the rag in a remaining top left tooth. If he worked his tongue under and rolled it up . . . Salt water came into his mouth. Was that good for the wound? Perhaps he'd die healed. There, he could just begin to suck in a little air from the left corner of his mouth by twisting his lips up. But, damn, they hurt. His mouth hurt. Well, he wasn't going to fall asleep this time, anyway.

There was no reason for Ginger to kill him—except that he was losing Ginger the chance of becoming very rich and maybe having lunch at the Maidstone Club, and Ginger was a very very sore loser and a very violent fellow, below his Eagle Scout skin, even unto pathology.

Thank God. Where have you been?

"You believe in god?" his father's ghost asked.

Do you believe in ghosts, Dad?

His father smiled. His father needed a shave. When he smiled the white bristles picked up the gleam off the water. "You got spirit, Leonard. I like that in you. And you're kind. But you never put your virtues where they could count."

You'll never forgive me being a cop.

"It's not me. Not me. History. History! You're on the wrong side. You're with the hegemony."

Hegemony? Dad, even *The Nation* doesn't use that word anymore.

"These people—Leonard, you thought you alone could change them? You're in over your head."

Almost over my head. A few more minutes. Dad, I love you. It's harder to remember Mom, she died so long ago, but I loved her. I love Karen very much. Do you know if she loves me?

"No. How should I? What do you think, I'm one of your literary ghosts? I'm me, me in you, Leonard. You know?"

I know. I know. "I know," Schwartz heard himself say out loud, the gag worked loose. But it filled his mouth with salt water and his father fled. Dying like this was crazy. Aggravating. No, it was *boring*. Boring! He couldn't hold his head up anymore.

"I'm dying of boredom," he said, in what sounded to him like a very sweet voice. He shut his left eye and felt the water come over his head.

"You have spirit."

What did his father want from him now?

His head was out, held. A big hand pulled his head up. He opened his left eye. "Soloff?"

"It was the torture, the pleasure he took. I don't like

you, you understand. You've cost my cause a great
deal. But I've had too much torture in my life to let . . ."
He took off the loosened gag and opened a Swiss army
knife.

"Wait, I don't want to fall in. I can't swim like this."

"Don't worry: it's only three or four feet deep here."

Soloff cut the ropes so that Schwartz's feet dropped
in. He held him under the arms and leaned him over the
gangplank and began working to free his hands.

"Will you speak up for me?" Soloff asked.

Schwartz looked into the beard. "I'll tell the whole
truth; this part should help, even though your real mo-
tive here is self preservation. Now you'd better tell me
some truths. Amboys, first," he said, and tried being
tough and spit. Nothing elegant, but what dribbled
down wasn't so completely blood.

"Yes, I will. But Whelehan has gone mad. It was
never a plan to kill you until this morning. He—"

"Amboys."

Using the knife, Soloff worked away at the knots. "I
was early that night, driving on Dune Road just about to
turn into Troost's. I saw Amboys walking down the road
in the pouring rain. But rather than coming up to
Troost's drive, he turned into the drive before, to the
east, where a big house was under construction. I wondered what he was doing, so I parked and followed him.
It was so windy out there—like a hurricane. I went up
the drive but I couldn't see anything until by the side of
the unfinished house I almost stepped on him. Amboys
was lying next to a big beam. I saw right away that it
had crushed his head. It must have slid down or blown
down from the floor above. Try to hold your hands still.

"So I listened for his breath, but of course he was
dead. I had the instinct to call Whelehan. I knew him,

I'd introduced him to Troost. So I drove back over the canal bridge to Quogue and called from a booth, but Whelehan had already left, because I wanted him at the meeting, maybe to convince Amboys. You understand. So I drove back and waited for him. And . . . Here, roll your wrists."

Schwartz's hands were free. They didn't even hurt, weren't even deeply marked. What a bugger Whelehan was. "So what then?"

"Whelehan came along soon and I had him park way at the front of Troost's drive and I took him to the body. Wait. Here." He helped Schwartz up to sit on the gangplank and began to work on the knots tight to his thighs, knees and ankles.

"Whelehan was very decisive. He went through Amboys's pockets, found the deed and told me we could use Amboys as he was to force Troost's allegiance and cooperation. I had my doubts, but he convinced me that Troost's fear and his being a policeman would do it. And he was right. Oh, and of course he said he'd need a bigger share of the profits. So he put the deed back in the pocket, and the two of us proceeded with his plan: we carried Amboys as if he was walking between us."

"And you never let Troost get close until after the faked argument and Whelehan pretending to kill him with the butt of his gun. The burial at Troost's was the final insurance."

"Yes."

"Yes. It fits. Ah, damn, my knees, my poor back of the knees. Shit. The ankles. I'm not going to think about what you might have done to Amboys if he'd been alive. Okay, so that's Amboys. I think you're in some trouble, fooling with a corpse like that, but the coroner's report should clear you of anything more seri-

ous—with Amboys. And, of course, Whelehan, that
crafty bastard, knew he hadn't murdered Amboys.
That's why he was so cocky even after Troost confessed. Oh, wow. All right. Another truth now, Vladimir. The mushrooms. No, keep untying me."

Soloff's shaggy head was bent over Schwartz's
ankles.

"I tell you, I don't honestly know any more. I remember my mixed feelings. My intense dislike for you
and my . . . This is the truth you want, so please . . ."

"Yes. Go on."

"I was so struck with Karen. I am impulsive in these
ways. Perhaps compulsive. It shames me, it disgusts
me, but . . . But I gathered mushrooms after you two had
gone without taking such care. Perhaps I broke off the
bottoms. I might have wished that you would be hurt,
but not die. But never, never that Karen or Natasha . . .
Ah, I was mildly ill, but then I am so used to wild
mushrooms and had not eaten many. And that is all I
know. There, you're untied. I'll help you stand."

Schwartz was wobbly. He let Soloff hold him up and
walked leaning on him to the door.

"And?" asked Soloff as they stood in the late afternoon sunshine.

Schwartz leaned against the doorjamb. "Natasha. A
few straight words about Natasha."

"She felt sorry for me with that poison ivy, and she
feels responsible to everyone for the best solution for
the land. So she first went to charm you from further
complicating the business of whose land it is. But then I
believe she came to like you very much. She took your
view on the land. A nice girl, but too emotional, perhaps. And that is the truth. Well?"

Schwartz touched his lips. They were split and swollen tender. His tongue found another tooth that would no doubt have to go. Every bit of him was sodden except his badge and credit card which survived to cost him.

"Well, thanks for coming back for me, Vladimir. The sun is good and life feels good, lucky for you. I have other questions, but they'll wait. Whelehan, I take it, has no idea you're here, so . . ."

"No. I believe he's suspicious. But he didn't follow."

"Where is he?"

"Now? I'm not sure. When we returned he said he needed to speak with Karen and . . ." Soloff stopped, looked at Schwartz and said, "No!"

"No, my ass!" said Schwartz, limping faster behind Soloff through the reeds. At least she'd have a rescue attempt by two men who loved her.

The satisfaction of that thought made him spit blood.

11

He followed Soloff back into the woods at the base of the hill, but at the root celler door leading to the tunnel he shook his head. If Whelehan were suspicious, he could trap them easily in there.

Schwartz sat on the ground and rubbed his legs. His mouth felt worse: swollen, tender, full of toothache and unrubbable. "Does Whelehan have other allies here, like the charming Wolf or the punk wolf cub?"

"No. Baldock is a minor investor in the development and knows Whelehan slightly, but he knows nothing of his—activities."

"Oh, damn, he'll still think Whelehan's a normal on-duty policeman. Have you told him any different?"

"No."

"Me neither. Damn. We'd better split up. You that way, me up here. I have to trust you. But you're no fool, Vladimir; you know you have to cooperate. See if you can find a gun, your shotgun, and let's meet in, say, twenty minutes in my little maple bedroom. It's so corny obvious a place that maybe Ginger won't think to look there. You know where it is?"

"Yes. I chose it for you," Soloff said, looking to the hills, from whence cameth no help.

"Way too late for coyness, Vladimir. I'll try to get to a phone. I'd arranged for support here, but it hasn't turned up. I'll try to get to Baldock. The vital thing is not to frighten Ginger if he's holding Karen or Natasha hostage. Nothing frontal. No heroics. If Ginger decides he doesn't like you, just go quietly; tell him what he wants to know. Bluff it out if you can, but no heroics. Yeah, I know: I've already said that. Are you all right, Soloff?"

Soloff nodded and disappeared up the hill.

Of course if Ginger were normal, he'd toss in his hand right now and cut his losses. But Ginger was a crazy player. He'd go on bluffing, raising the stakes and, who knows, maybe try to overturn the whole table. He might have convinced everyone up at the Manor House that it was he, Schwartz, who was crazy. Schwartz the rogue New York cop no one actually knew about. So why didn't they all take their shotguns and scythes and have a little look round? And if Ginger thought Soloff had deserted him, he'd say the same of him. It was too late to worry Soloff with these details. Schwartz moved off to come up behind the house from the northeast to see what he could see.

A shotgun. He could see Wolf with a shotgun in his hands and field glasses around his neck. Schwartz lay behind a shed on the edge of a field below the house. Wolf, in camouflage, was looking through the glasses now as if born to this sort of butlery; he lacked only his Panzer Division.

No, that's what I lack, Schwartz thought, seeing stout Sissy all in white roll up to Wolf, gun in hand, like Goering saying "Hi" to Rommel. Maybe if he went around to the front—

"What!" He rolled.

It was Karen, crouched behind him with a shotgun across her knees. A sight for sore everythings. He crawled back and pulled her down and kissed her. It was very painful.

"What's happened to you? Who's done this?"

"Wipe your mouth, sweetheart," he said Bogartly. "There's some of my split lip still on it. But don't you know what's happened? Isn't that why you have the shotgun, you genius?"

"No. I couldn't just hang around, so half an hour after you left lunch I went to the studio, and when no one was there or anywhere else I became frightened and took this because I thought you or I might need it. I've been hiding out here ever since. I can't even shoot this thing."

"Never mind. Whelehan tried to drown me, with your painter friend's aid, but Vladimir happily had second thoughts. Now Whelehan seems to have reappeared

to convince everyone that I'm the villain they should go
for."

"And where's the great Gallagher?"

"Ah, yes—a central, though apparently metaphysi-
cal question. The important thing is that you're a genius
to have thought of the gun. Where are the shells?"

"Shells?"

"Well, half a genius. At least it's one less gun for the
badly misled up there."

"I'm sorry, Len. I couldn't resist. I left two boxes of
shells in the shed there."

"This very shed behind which we crouch?"

"I'm a full genius again, right?"

"Right. Do you love me?"

"Blackmailer. Here: why not hold the gun and ask?"

Schwartz took the shotgun. It was a fine shotgun but
it was Vladimir's. If he asked her how she knew where
to find it, would that spoil his chances for a loving answer? "Karen, I've decided that you love me. Condi-
tionally, provisionally. So . . ."

He looked back to the terrace. A figure in bright yellow silk wearing a wide white pirate sash had joined the
Wehrmacht High Command. The figure also wore a
Second World War leather aviator's cap and carried what
from the distance appeared to be a pair of matched,
silver handled dueling pistols, antebellum 1860. They
were probably half cocked and it was probably Baldock.

"Karen, darling, we can't take them on. They're all
armed, a few of them intelligently. Look, what else is in
the shed? Hand grenades? Rocket launchers?"

"It's full of those clay pigeon things and those things
that . . . pigeon launchers. What is it, Len?"

"It's thinking. I'm thinking. I'm known as the cop
who thinks and you can watch . . . Okay, I'm done."

"It looked wonderful, you fool. What did it come up with?"

"I need your help. And you'll have to be damned brave for about five or ten minutes. But you'll be safe; things will only sound bad. We're going to sneak into this shed, load up some traps and then, in full view of the household up there, you'll throw and I'll shoot clay pigeons."

"And you're known as the *thinking* cop? Oh. Oh, wait. I get it. That's good. That's scary but good."

"You're wearing those shorts."

"Officer, I thought you'd never notice. Get your hands off. Your idea is that Baldock will see you're not what Whelehan says. You're a gentleman eccentric. He likes your class act and defects to your side. But until that wonderful moment, how do we stay alive?"

"I'm sure that nothing up there can hit us at this range. So even if they should fire . . . And another thing. Everyone else will come to watch, so it'll make a fine distraction during which maybe Soloff can find Whelehan or a phone, or maybe my reinforcements will arrive. Let's go; there's not much good light left and they'd better see that it's me."

"Me too."

Getting inside the shack unseen proved easy. Finding the discs and the trap and the shells proved easy. It was walking out the door into the field which proved a great uneasiness.

He said, "Ready if you are."

She said, "Ready. Len, do you love me?"

He said, "Unprovisionally, unconditionally."

The first five feet were terrible. Neither dared look toward the house. Then he did. Wolf was handing the binoculars to Baldock and pointing in their direction.

Baldock was fiddling around with his leather cap.

"At least they can't see us tremble from there," he said.

"I'm glad you said that. That makes me feel so much calmer. Let's go. Over there?"

When he nodded she went forward a few yards and calmly took her position.

Schwartz set down the clay discs and regarded the trap. "The other way, darling. It's aimed right for my kneecaps. That's it, there, so they fly out over the field. You just press your foot down each time I yell 'pull.'"

"Shouldn't that be 'press'?"

Schwartz loaded the gun. The department had made him fire this sort of thing a few times. But never at clay discs. He heard shouting from the terrace and yelled, "Pull!"

Out it flew. He sighted, led and pulled a trigger. Missed.

"Pull!" he yelled again. It flew out, lifted in his sight. He led and pulled the other trigger. The clay split over the field.

Reloading, he saw figures running on the terrace toward the group at its edge. He winked at Karen. He snapped close the gun. There was a shot from the house. Karen ducked.

"Don't let it bother you. This is the scary part I told you about, but keep a stiff upper foot and keep pulling."

Karen smiled. "May I say something?"

"What?"

"Oi."

"That's the stuff. Pull! Pull!"

One disc exploded. Then another.

Karen said, "Darling, I hope John Baldock is as impressed with this as you are."

Shotgun fire came from the terrace. Schwartz reloaded. "If he's half as impressed, we're in like Flynn." He wished he hadn't said that. Flynn made him think of Gallagher who wasn't there or didn't care or—

The sound of a strange little shot. There was Baldock, a pistol up in the air. Had it been bad aim or a good sign?

"Pull! Pull!" Schwartz yelled. He got the first, missed the second. "Not bad shooting for a half-drowned fellow with a smashed-in mouth. By the way, did you call me 'darling' a minute ago?"

"I may have, I was so scared."

"And now?"

"I'm about to wet my pretty shorts. How much more of this, Len?"

"I love you madly. I'm going to turn to the gallery, hopefully not the shooting gallery, and wave in a cheerful yet elegantly haughty manner. Do I look elegantly haughty?"

"Like a car window washer at the corner of Bowery and Houston, darling."

Schwartz ran his hand through his hair. His hair was horrid; it ran its fingers back through him. But the open barrel of the shotgun hung gracefully, his hand waved slowly through the air with bonhomie and his smile was absolute Cary Grant, if Grant had thick split lips and a bloody mouth with teeth knocked out.

"Well?" Karen asked.

"Well," he said, putting his nonchalant hand into his sodden trouser pocket, "the good news is that there's no red hair among the entranced throng up there."

"The bad?"

"Is that they're maybe not entranced. But all eyes are on us and so we have a choice, my little duck. Either

you take the shotgun and we walk arm in arm to our
charming host, our fellow guests and helpful staff . . ."

"Yes? Or?"

"Or we take off all our clothes, these lendings, and
do the deed of descending dusk right here."

"Oh, Len. Oh, Len."

"Yes, yes?"

"I'll take the shotgun."

"Ah, yes. Well, it was only an idea. Put mostly," he
said as they began their walk across the field, "to relax
you."

"I don't know that it did. On the other hand, it certainly didn't excite me. We're coming into range, aren't
we, sweet?"

"Think not of that, my dabchick, my dove, my pretty
puller of clay pigeons. Think rather that in a few moments you'll be sipping a cool gin and tonic, this will
seem but a sordid dream and you'll be the admiration of
all."

"Promise?" she said, squeezing the arm on which her
hand rested.

"Of course."

"Who's up there? I can't look."

"Besides our bizarre host, who is, yes, he's smiling!
Besides our delightful host, there are the former Bundeswehr Bund, all of whom are now sundowning in
Brooks Brothers, and the butler, lupine and svelte as
ever, and, yes, the slobbering underbutler Sid Viscous,
and—keep walking, my pet—and the ageless nanny
ycleped Sissy, who ain't afraid of nothing, and also as-
sorted clowns, rustics and spear carriers. And it isn't so
far to go now, Karen. We're all right."

He tried to keep the pace steady. Where was Whelehan? His heart was thumping and he didn't want to look up at the windows because . . .

He said, "Then, there's the interesting who's not there. Whelehan's not there; Soloff's not there. Not also there is La Lawless, nor there is Gallagher neither, nor is he out of hell, as far as I'm concerned."

"Natasha?"

"Ah. No. Now that you remind me—no. Maybe Vladimir has spirited her off to safety. And now, my good angel, I shall address this gathered multitude." He shouted, "Hello up there! What's happening? Some historical pageant you're putting on, John? Lord Byron at Peenemünde?"

"You two have style. You are originals," Baldock shouted down. "Come, come now. Madame is due down soon and we must all be there with drinkies before dinner."

Schwartz nudged Karen. "Hear that?"

"You are clever, and thanks for all that foolish talk. It helped."

"Aw, I'll bet you say that to every toothless hero who happens by."

They walked up the steps. Baldock had stuck the old dueling pistols into his white sash. "Sorry, you two, to be such a rotten host. Simply collapsed this morning. And then, I am *so* embarrassed, that silly policeman convinced me and *tout ensemble* that you were up to no good. Hence the little home guard regiment was mustered. Such an injustice I've done you. Might a bit of champagne move you to forgive, hmm?"

Schwartz shook the shells in his pocket. No, they couldn't walk around with a loaded shotgun. Even in this place, someone would comment. "Very kind, John. You understand, Sergeant Whelehan's—unwell." He touched the side of his head. "But what would hit the spot right now is a bit of freshen-up for both of us."

"Oh, my dears! But of course. How stupid of me. Go, go, of course. But do hurry so that we're all together at the foot of the stairs at six—for Madame. Such fun! You haven't met yet. I promise you will *adore* . . . But, there, I'm keeping you again."

As they walked off Schwartz felt Karen's arm tremble on his. She was looking up at some windows. He saw nothing.

"Something moved. Someone . . . I couldn't make out who. But whoever, I thought . . . The figure seemed naked. Maybe I didn't see anything."

12

Maybe, but alone, their Nora and Nick euphoria escaped them, leaving Karen flat with the fear of being alone even in the bathroom and Schwartz with a stale dry mouth, glass after glass of water.

He watched Karen shower with a sense of being forever too dirty to touch her. He said the figure in the window was most likely a houseguest or a servant, changing.

"You're saying that so I won't be frightened."

"Leave the shower running for me. Yes. I don't want you or anyone else here frightened. It won't help."

He lost his breath in the shower steam and a headache stabbed like broken glass. Afterward, he looked in the mirror and saw the mess he felt.

What would help, Karen told him, her head into the bathroom, would be his accompanying her downstairs to be with the others, that is, if he could stop staring at himself in the mirror.

"What is it? You were pleased with me five minutes ago."

"Protective adrenaline. It suddenly occurred to me that I was being grateful for your saving me from the jeopardy you created, like the woman thanking the man who's stopped hitting her."

Schwartz remembered the photos of Jean Whelehan. He'd never . . . He said, "I'll take you downstairs because I think you'll be safest in a group that doesn't include me. Then I'll have a quick look for Ginger and the others, including my Shinnecock pals, who seem to have changed their minds about helping."

Karen said she couldn't blame them.

Back on his own upstairs, Schwartz considered what he might have meant by a quick look. A forty three room mansion with secret doors and hidden passageways. Ten minutes to showtime and he'd have a quick look. The randomness of his endeavor overcame him, and he found himself back in the small maple bedroom. There were Karen's underpants on his bed.

It wasn't necessary. None of this was necessary. He saw that. Truth or the law had little to do with it—justice less. Yes, there was the Johnson kid, but against everything else? Eight minutes now; he'd visit the scene of the crime against his mouth.

The studio door was ajar. Schwartz looked through the hinge crack. No one. He'd made this mess and now

he'd have to clean it up. He went to the portrait of
Karen.

He sighed. Of course she had to fall in love with
someone who could paint her like this. He couldn't destroy it and he couldn't afford it, even if he had the
money to buy it. Soloff's vision.

He saw the small door to the right and went in. Yes,
this was the place, a small storeroom, and that would be
the door down. Such a great house for Ghosts or Murder
in the Dark. His heart was pounding as he opened the
door. Well, in for a penny, in for a pounding.

Darkness at the start of the stairs. A faintly sweet
smell as of perfume or vanishing cream, and not only
stairs but passageways between the walls right and left.
Vanishing cream. Where was Whelehan? A waste of
time.

Turning, Schwartz saw the blue cloth in the corner of
the storeroom covering what looked like an easel. That
blue reminded him . . .

He pulled it off and stood looking at a painting for
some moments. Then he shook his head, covered it and
went downstairs.

One minute after six in the great hall of Baldock
Manor House. Three gentlemen from New Orleans,
Karen and Schwartz, and Wolf and unterWolf attending,
stood grouped at the bottom of the walnut staircase that
rose to a landing and swept up to the balustraded gallery.

John Unicorn Baldock, having hushed everyone, was
at a wall panel. He pressed a button. Gentle music
played: "Stars Fell on Alabama." Schwartz couldn't believe this. Baldock winked at him. Was it a joke? Baldock turned a knob. The staircase flooded with pale

light. It had to be a joke. Or did it? Did Baldock think he was von Stroheim or someone wilder?

Karen moved close and whispered, "Moonlight, starlight," as upstairs right a door swung open and Miss Perdita Lawless began a slow glide down.

For half a second he caught it: her gown of silver lamé, little moons ashimmer on an elegant slim figure . . .

Schwartz looked down into his orange juice. No one was laughing, but wasn't it supposed to be a giggle? Was she nuts? Was Baldock hosting a pleasant cocktail party or the theater of cruelty?

He looked up. Perdita Lawless was at the central landing, where the trick of distance didn't work, where she was no ingenue but eighty if a day and her bony hips stuck from the gown like a hanger had fallen to its waist. And her tight and lineless, manufactured face looked even older than the wrinkled skin that sagged under her arm.

She moved onto the landing, center stage, and for the first time looked down, not really at the group below but at some forever fixed audience she saw behind with such intensity that Schwartz half turned to see who—

Karen nudged him. At the back of the landing a walnut panel was sliding open. Natasha's head came out with an arm around her neck. Then she was pushed out. The arm was Whelehan's. He held a gun behind her ear, and as they moved forward into the light Schwartz saw the blood from her nose and her right eye swollen yellow and purple, shut to a slit. Someone gasped.

And Perdita Lawless, unaware of the tableau behind her, took it for a gasp of admiration and tilted her head shyly, a girl at her first formal ball.

Karen whispered, "Do something!"

Schwartz looked. Whelehan was confused, crazed. He was nearly choking Natasha, looking about him as if lost. A sneeze could set him off.

"What should I do, shoot him with my finger? And you wouldn't want me risking my life to save Natasha, of all people."

She whispered, "Says who?" and kicked his shin. "I don't like her, but she's a woman, damn you, and she's worth five of him and two of you." She kicked him again.

Biting his sore lip to keep from crying out made him cry out, "Ouch! Damn! Shh. Okay, I'll try."

But Whelehan moved first. Banging Natasha's head with the side of his gun, he shouted, "Move, bitch!"

At the word "bitch," Perdita Lawless began a slow burn, magnificent turn. Her old hands came onto her silver hips. "Who," she said. "Who," she repeated in the grandest *dame* voice, "do you imagine you're calling a bitch, you flaming asshole?"

There was nothing Schwartz could do. He felt Karen's hand dig into his arm as he watched Whelehan point the gun past Natasha at the lost Perdita. Whelehan moved closer, pushing Natasha as his shield. Shadows in the gallery? No, too late.

"You," Whelehan said and stopped. He moved out from behind Natasha and held his gun at the end of his straight arm toward Perdita's contemptuous face.

Schwartz saw the trigger hand go tense. Then it relaxed. "Wait," he said, open mouthed. "I know you. You're Perdi—"

A line appeared through Whelehan's cheeks as her name became a scream. The gun dropped. He fell. Screams, whoops. A naked figure leapt onto Whelehan from the gallery above as he kept screaming, clutching the arrow through his cheeks. Perdita screamed.

The man next to Schwartz screamed, "Indians! Indians! We're surrounded by braves!"

Schwartz screamed, "No, no, don't!" running up to the landing, but the flash of metal had come and gone. Whelehan's hands went from his cheeks to the top of his head. He screamed once more and passed out.

Schwartz stared at the young man in buckskin loincloth with sweet smelling five-and-ten war paint on his face. Then he stared at the blood that dripped from the scalp the young man held by its ginger hair.

"Oh, just look," said someone below. "Look at all of them, and would you look at those little outfits?"

Karen was on the landing comforting Natasha as Schwartz pushed through the Shinnecock war party. "Police, Miss Lawless. You're a brave woman; that man was very dangerous."

She scowled at him. "Brave? Brave, my ass, buster. No one, but *no one* upstages me!"

EPILOGUE

At Gallagher's Bash

"It sounds to me," said Bill McNulty, "like a mix between *Sunset Boulevard* and *Geronimo*." He turned to the girl with the tray and took a miniature pizza and a pink paper napkin. McNulty was short and thin and had wiry salt-and-pepper hair and the pale gray eyes of a Weimaraner. He was a film buff and Deputy Commissioner of Administration.

As McNulty moved off to have a word with Kitty Gallagher, Schwartz said, "In retrospect, it seems more like a camp version of *Animal Crackers*." But it didn't and he disliked the distortion in his wisecrack.

Schwartz stood by the dock at the bottom of the lawn trying to guess the numbers. A hundred, easily. More like two or three? He counted people on the lower slope: fifty. So, yes, at least two fifty.

Gallagher's end of the season bash was crowded with flowered dresses, green golf pants, blue madras plaid jackets and neckties with little spouting whales. It had a clam bar made of ice blocks, college girl waitresses, hot hors d'oeuvres and three bars with everything. It was some bash. Some bore. Why was he drinking Tab? It was terrible. He could drink again; he'd promised him-

239

self a real drink once he'd decided to come.

Karen had insisted. Karen had been very insistent
since Baldock Island that he pursue his career and her,
or that she pursue him. Her call to Gallagher had been
amazingly insistent: her demands of what the department owed him—the dentistry, the boat, their formal
thanks, the lost guns. And Gallagher, laughing, agree-
ing to everything but the guns; Karen then screaming
her insistence and Gallagher saying he'd try, okay, he'd
try. Karen had put the phone down, said, "Finished!"
and added, "And that includes Natasha." Very insistent.
He didn't like to think of it as the insistence of guilt,
expert as he was in that field.

Where was Karen? Lost up there in the heavy crowd,
doubtless charming the heavies, winning the hearts and
minds of police officials and city officials and state officials down from Albany, and the lawyers and developers
who were here, oh yes, and even the priests. Yes, why
were there so many priests? They weren't all relatives.

So Gallagher had come through with everything—
even a special citation for Schwartz from Albany, which
he refused. Karen had lifted her eyebrows, had seen his
scowl and had put her eyebrows back down again. She
said she understood.

Damned Gallagher and his festival of publicity—
those pals of his on the *News*. HAMPTONS LAND
SCAM, GIVE IT BACK TO THE INDIANS, and even
CROOKED COP IN BIG L.I. SWINDLE had worked
out well. Gallagher was seen to be rooting out the rot,
even when the rot was related. No mention, of course,
of Schwartz refusing a citation, no story there. But there
was a big story in the shock revelation of the silent
partner. Gallagher decided to tell him the day before it

broke in all three papers. Schwartz had just come back from dental work.

"Come in, Lenny. How'd it go? Hey, no shit, the teeth look great."

"Thanks, Tom. How's your nephew?"

"Whelehan?"

"Yeah, sharp guess, that nephew."

"He's pulling through okay. He'll stand trial, and I'm pressing the D.A.'s office out there to throw the book at him. So you see, I was stringing him along all the time."

"Ah, the Danton *and* the Robespierre of Homicide. Well, why not? You know his lawyers will get a reduced responsibility plea, and with their helpful information and his sterling record he'll end up doing a year or two in a ward at Pilgrim State, come out, move and probably end up in another lucky police force where he'll rebuild all his careers. Shit."

"Maybe. I don't know. I want to level with you, Lenny. All along I haven't been able to explain the Albany involvement because you can guess how my hands were tied. But honest to God, if I had, it wouldn't have made no difference to what happened."

"So?" Schwartz asked from over by the window. Down below in the plaza, the Chinese fast-food truck was doing a great business, the Italian only so-so. "So?"

"So you might like to know that none other than Barry Sutherland is up to his neck in it. Barry Sutherland. I mean millions invested behind Troost's land grab. Sutherland—you know, runs the Republican Party machine out there, and that county's been Republican for a hundred years. Hey! Lenny the Lefty, I'm talking to you. I thought that would please you. Jesus."

It hadn't pleased him. He'd put his life and Karen's

at risk for a political favor, one more political favor
Gallagher was doing, probably for some other Republican in Albany, not that it mattered. A small vendetta.
Some other Sutherland would replace Sutherland. He
asked Gallagher to please stop treating him like a
schoolboy or a jerk. He was ashamed of himself.
Ashamed. And ashamed, damn it, for Gallagher!

Some case. Shit! Troost would probably go free for
his cooperativeness. Whelehan, they'd agreed, would
look at pine trees from the nuthouse windows for a
while, and Soloff—the valiant prince Vladimir, who'd
retired from the fray and hidden in the Baldock woods
until everything was safe—well, they wouldn't bring
charges on the famous anti-Communist just for taking a
short walk on the beach with an old stiff.

Gallagher pointed out that Schwartz had saved the
land.

"The land? Those poor Indians won't get a look in,
deeds or no deeds. This whole country is based on not
honoring those deeds. You know what'll happen? Sure
you do. The old Russians will pop off soon and their
kids will fall over themselves rushing to develop that
land. They'll probably use Phil Troost!"

Gallagher had muttered that Schwartz was never satisfied, and that's when Schwartz had said he'd be satisfied at this point with no citation. "No fucking Albany
errand-boy citation."

"Hello there. You look lost in thought. I'm Father
Bernard."

"Hi." The party hummed back around him. "I'm Len
Schwartz."

"Ah. Yes, you're not . . . You're, ah, of the Hebrew
persuasion?"

"Hebrew persuasion? Is that anything like Catholic pride and prejudice?"

Someone was tapping his arm. Father Bernard seemed to see someone he had to speak with and excused himself.

"Okay, Len. Calm down. It's okay, darling. Here. It's all right for you to have one now." Karen handed him a drink.

Schwartz stood with the Tab in one hand and the gin and tonic in the other. He looked at Karen's short blue skirt and baggy blue jacket. She was beautiful. He put down the Tab.

"Go on," she said. "It might make you a little tipsy, that's all."

"Yes? I could use a little tipsy now. This party—"

"Don't, please. It's a nice party. Remember? We all have to go to nice parties when we're grown up and have real jobs. So here's to—to a nice end of the season bash."

He lifted the glass. It tasted very good, very coolly juniper.

Karen was smiling. "I see you're in a very preppy sweater."

"You may not believe this, ma'am, but I'm old enough to have a son at Yale who keeps me in J. Press, when his allowance allows. And may I say how very well you look in that particular blue? It suits you, sets off your looks. You're of the dark Irish persuasion, I believe?

"Up there, a few minutes ago, someone thought I was Spanish."

"Yes," he said. "I can see that. It's the blue—like the blouse in Vladimir's portrait of you. That's such a good painting!"

"Yes. Yes, it's good. He does have a special quality:
the brushstrokes . . ."

"Like Goya."

"Goya? No, I don't think so." She looked at him in
an ordinary way. "What makes you say that?"

He couldn't hold her gaze. "I don't know." He didn't
want to know. But he knew, he'd seen, she knew the
reference to Goya . . . She and Soloff . . . He wouldn't
name it; if he named it to himself it would be real. He
took a drink. Through the glass Karen was a soft blue
shimmer, like the blouse in her portrait or like the cloth
he'd taken off the painting in the storeroom, that other
Soloff portrait in which the blue was the background on
which Karen lay naked, her mouth in that deep smile
he'd been the only . . . Yes, Karen to the life.

Schwartz lowered his glass. Of course all that about
her being his mother was nonsense. She was his wife,
his friend, this *maja* who smiled at him with clear and
open eyes.

ABOUT THE AUTHOR

IRVING WEINMAN was born in Boston in 1937. He has two children and he lives with the writer Judith Kazantzis in London and Key West, Florida. This is his second novel.